Praise for *The Grimmelings*

'A compelling, lovir
liminal spaces (of
folkloric fusion. Rac
breathe. Her dialogu
new perspectives in
world that is familiar
with flashes of beauty.'

— DAVID MITCHELL, *CLOUD ATLAS, THE BONE CLOCKS*

'One of those very rare books that feels like it has always existed, as if the world has been holding space for this story. With wonderfully assured writing, this is Susan Cooper for the next generation. King writes with the utmost respect for her readers, for the story and for language itself.'

— ZANA FRAILLON, *THE BONE SPARROW, THE RAVEN'S SONG*

'I was gripped until the very end and it left me in tears — which is always the sign of a cracking good book. The writing just sings; it's evocative and atmospheric with the moodiness of *Wuthering Heights*. And the horse action is epically good! I completely loved this book! Totally genius.'

— STACY GREGG, *THE PRINCESS AND THE FOAL*

'A dynamic new adventure that will reverberate in the reader's memory . . . playing with words in the most skilful way, exploring the language of horses, of winds, of landscapes, of relationships.'

— *NEW ZEALAND LISTENER*

'A tense tale of animal companionship, wild magic, and the majesty and awe nature inspires.'

— *SYDNEY MORNING HERALD*

The GRIMMELINGS

RACHAEL KING

GUPPY
BOOKS

THE GRIMMELINGS
is a GUPPY BOOK

First published in Australia and New Zealand by Allen & Unwin 2024

First published in the UK in 2024 by
Guppy Books,
Bracken Hill,
Cotswold Road,
Oxford OX2 9JG

978-1-916558-250

1 3 5 7 9 10 8 6 4 2

Papers used by Guppy Books are from well-managed
forests and other responsible sources.

GUPPY PUBLISHING LTD Reg. No. 11565833

A CIP catalogue record for this book is available from the British Library.

Printed and bound in Great Britain by CPI Books Ltd

For my mother Ros Henry
and
for all the Scottish grannies

'We all live our lives dangerously, in a state of jeopardy, at the edge of calamity. You have discovered that the veil that separates your ordered life from disarray is wafer thin.'

— NICK CAVE, FROM THE FILM
THIS MUCH I KNOW TO BE TRUE (2022)

1

Grimmelings: the first and last
glimmers of light in the day

The same evening Josh Underhill went missing, the black horse appeared on the hill above the house.

It was Ella's favourite time of day, when magic could happen: the sky a deep indigo, bleeding to pink at the horizon, and the last of the mauve light draining from the land. The grimmelings. As she stood upstairs at her bedroom window, Ella could just make out her piebald pony Magpie and the other horses moving around the paddock contentedly.

She opened the window and leaned out.

'Maggieee!'

An answering whinny from Magpie carried on the breeze and settled inside her like a promise. Tomorrow they would ride.

The first star hung bright and low over the horizon. Ella took a deep breath, inhaling the crisp air. She should make a wish. But what would it be? Nothing so big as asking for her father back, or for her gran, Grizzly, not to die. That was the same wish she made nearly every night when she glimpsed Venus in the sky. Something simpler.

A friend.

She'd like a friend for the school holidays, so she didn't have to be alone.

Beyond the paddock, a chattering disturbance erupted in the sky. A cloud of birds reeled in the air, darkened shapes barely visible against the coming night, making it seem alive, a pulsing shadow. She couldn't tell from here what kind of birds they were but she'd never seen a flock behave like that before.

Another movement caught her eye. Outlined against the light on the lower slopes of the Ben, the great hill that overlooked the property: another horse. Not one of their own. It moved restlessly, back and forth, then stopped. It was just a shape, really, but she sensed it: a dark horse, with power in its muscles, half unlocking a memory that stayed just out of reach.

The bird cloud hovered above as if waiting, holding its breath. The dull ache that had been in her lower belly all day flared and she heard her own voice in her head: *You're cursed, Josh Underhill.*

Ella jerked back from the window. She didn't know where the horse had come from or who it belonged to, but she got the distinct feeling it had been watching the house, watching *her*. She closed the curtains, shutting it out.

As she came down the stairs, her mother's phone rang.

'Hello?' Her mother flicked a tea towel over her shoulder. 'Oh, Raewyn, hi. What's up?' Her voice was stiff. The locals never rang Morag for a chat, or for anything friendly, really. 'No, I haven't seen him. I'll ask them.' She took the phone from her ear. 'Girls, did you see Josh Underhill after school at all?'

Ella and her little sister Fiona looked at each other. 'Yes, he was on the bus.'

What they didn't say was that they'd been glad to get off it, away from Josh and his honking voice. He'd tried to trip Fiona as they walked down the aisle, even though she was only half his size.

'Get lost, *dafty*,' Ella had called back to him, channelling Grizzly. Josh had grinned at her with a puzzled look, so she'd tried again: 'Go jump in the lake!'

'Whatya gonna do?' Josh sneered. 'Put a curse on me? Get your gran to do it? Or your mum? My dad says you're a house of witches and you can't pay your rent.' He nudged the kid next to him, who wriggled away and refused to look at anyone.

'Yes,' said Ella, turning as she followed Fiona off the bus. 'That's exactly what I'm going to do.' She pointed at him. 'You're cursed, Josh Underhill. Better watch out!'

She felt uneasy at the memory.

'Did you see him after that maybe?' asked Morag.

'No. Why?' said Fiona.

Morag held up one finger — wait — and went back to Raewyn. 'No, they didn't see him after the bus. What does Susan think happened to him? Does he have any friends he might have gone to see? Yes, of course you have. I'm so sorry. Let us know what we can do.'

She hung up.

'What is it?' asked Ella. But she knew. *You're cursed*.

'Josh has gone missing. They're sending out a search party.'

And just like that, a shiver of darkness descended on the Basin.

2

Gurling: the howling of wind
Huffling: wind blowing in sudden
gusts

'Josh didn't come home after school,' Morag went on. 'His mum's beside herself. It's shaping up to be a cold night and she's worried he's fallen in a ditch somewhere. Raewyn and some others are ringing everyone they can think of for her. I'll go out and join the search party. You'll have to have an early night.'

'But I need to have a bath,' said Fiona.

'Ach, Fi-*ona*.' Ella rolled her eyes. 'It won't kill you not to have a bath one night of your life. Can't you think of anyone else but yourself for a change?'

Fiona closed her eyes. Ella could tell that she was counting, trying not to lose her cool.

5

'Fine,' said Morag. 'I'll run you a bath now. But it's in and out, and then to bed with a book, okay? I don't want Grizzly having to get up and look after you.'

They disappeared up the stairs to the bathroom.

Ella opened the back door and went outside into the new night. The wind had died down but it was still cold. More stars were popping out. Soon the sky would be awash with them. On moonless nights like this, Ella and her dad used to lie on top of the car up on the Ben, bundled up in blankets, holding hands as whole armies of shooting stars streaked by, or the slow steady beeline of satellites went about their business. The galaxies were like clouds, the sky huge and open and cacophonous, and Ella a small dot on a small dot below. She missed those nights, when down here everything felt ordered and right but a veil shimmered above them, with calamity just on the other side.

There wasn't much time for stargazing these days.

Ella turned and looked up to where Morag was bathed in the yellow light of the bathroom, helping Fiona out of the bath. She watched as they disappeared from the window, replaced by a black square when the light went out.

* * *

'CLOSE THE DOOR quickly, lassie,' said Ella's grandmother when she came inside. 'You'll bring the ghosts in. Then come and give yer nan a kiss.' Grizzly sat on the couch by the fire with her feet up, her legs covered with a blanket and a crossword puzzle in her lap.

Ella threw herself down beside her, curling her legs up and leaning in for the kiss. Ella and Fiona called her Grizzly not because she complained a lot, but because her name was Griselda, and they all preferred it to Nan. She was Scottish, and it suited her.

'Oop careful, girl, of my words book, won't you.'

Ella pulled out a battered leather notebook from under her and put it on the low table in front of the couch, next to an apple core and two empty coffee mugs.

'Don't you worry, I'm sure that lad hasn't gone far. Now tell me, did you use the words I gave you?'

'Not out loud, but I memorised them.' Ella reached into the pocket of her jeans and pulled out the folded scrap of paper she had found by her porridge that morning. It had two words and their definitions on it: *gurling* and *huffling*.

Grizzly was a self-described word-hoard. She collected words like other people collected old coins or pottery owls. Most of them described nature, and most of them were from Scotland, but she collected other

7

words that took her fancy as well. She said that words native to New Zealand, her new home, helped bind her to the place.

She kept them in the leather notebook (her *grimoire*, she called it, a book of spells) and left them for Ella on slips of paper pushed under her door, or in the bathroom by the toothbrushes. Once inside her riding boot, which she only found later, stuck to her sock. Words such as *roke* for the mist that rose up like smoke from the damp ground on a cold autumn morning, or the *mizzle* that was more like a mist than a rain. Kapua, a Māori word, was a bank of clouds.

Grizzly had taught her all the words for the different winds. The stour-wind was the wind of a driving storm that brought with it pelting rain and black, smouldering cloud. On an otherwise still day, a whiffle was nothing more than the light breath you feel on your cheek before a kiss. The Nor'wester scudded in great gasping gusts, gurling and huffling; it could knock you off your feet. Ella's grandad's dinghy was found dancing on the lake during a Nor'wester, with nobody inside. A week went by before he washed up on the shore.

Today's wind was lazy — so-named because it can't be bothered to go around you, so cuts right through to your bones instead. When they'd got off the bus Ella

8

and Fiona had pulled their coats tighter; Fiona's face, screwed up like a piece of paper, was barely visible under the hood of her yellow raincoat.

Ella cuddled closer to her grandmother and closed her eyes.

Grizzly's cancer had come back, and she spent most days on the couch in the big open-plan living area, too tired to move. Grizzly tried to hide it, but Ella knew she was also in a lot of pain most of the time. Before she got sick, she used to look after the girls while their mother worked, but now they had to employ Rita, a nurse from the town, to come and look after *her*.

At least she still had her words.

The phone rang again, and her mother came down the stairs, murmuring a few soft words to the caller before hanging up and bustling around, getting her coat and boots. The kettle was roaring, about to boil, and a thermos flask stood next to it.

Ella thought she hated Josh Underhill, but the small thrill that had run through her when she heard he was missing had been quickly replaced by deep shame. What if something really had happened to him? What if he'd been kidnapped, or worse? What if some animal had got him, or he'd been hit by a car? What if — and even inside her head she whispered the thought, in case it came true

— what if she had brought this on him by cursing him? She saw his big leering face then, the cruel teeth bared in a malignant smile.

Ella got up and went to her mother, who was pouring coffee into the thermos. 'I want to come with you.'

'I need you here to look after Fiona,' her mother said without looking up.

'Grizzly's here.'

'Grizzly is sick,' said Morag. 'It's not fair on her to leave her with Fiona.'

'I don't mind, I'll be good.' Fiona had appeared sitting halfway down the stairs, a pale shadow in a paler dressing gown. Now that she'd had her bath, she was calm, and the reality of a missing boy had sunk in. 'You have to find Josh.'

You don't even like Josh, Ella wanted to say, but she stopped herself. For all Fiona was inward-looking, she felt the pain of others acutely. Now, her voice was wobbly, and her eyes held a glint of tears. 'Please find him, Ellie. What if something bad's happened to him?'

Ella couldn't bear the thought of her own terrible visions plaguing Fiona too, taking on life, growing big and solid, invading her dreams.

But Morag was having none of it. 'I need you to be responsible for a change, Ella. You were supposed to help me rug up the horses earlier, remember? I had to do it myself. And don't think I didn't see you doubling Fi on that pony of yours. I know Magpie's a kitten with you, but she's unpredictable, and you need to show your sister consideration for her safety. And with no bridle! What were you thinking? It could have been a disaster.'

Ella said nothing. She found it was better to let her mother burn herself out than try and argue. It was true that Ella had coaxed Fi into riding with her to avoid the long walk from the bus in the cold wind, but Magpie had moved too quickly and Fi's fingers, stiff with fear, had become tangled in her mane. Their mother had come out of the house, drying her hands on a small towel while Ella was trying to help her off.

'What's going on?' she asked.

The sound of her voice snapped Fi out of her trance and she let go, squirming, so both girls oozed to the ground, unhurt. When Morag opened the gate, Fiona tumbled through and ran inside the house.

'What's wrong with her?'

Ella felt darkness descend on her face. 'What's ever wrong with her?' The meanness pinched at her mouth.

At that moment Magpie, who had been shuffling from hoof to hoof, flattened her tiny ears and stretched out her neck, teeth bared, towards Morag, but her mother was quick. She flicked her hand towel towards the pony's nose and growled.

'Don't even think about it, you little devil,' she hissed, her voice low and menacing. Magpie snapped her head back, wheeled around and trotted indignantly away.

Morag had come inside later and banged around, tidying up, while Ella hid in her room. They never knew whether their mother only did housework when she was angry, or whether it was the housework itself that made her angry — whatever it was, the girls stayed well out of her way. In some ways it was a relief to have the sea wall of her anger break.

'Honestly, Ellie, you're all over the place.' Morag was still busy in the kitchen, roughly pushing around the pile of dinner dishes on the bench. 'Please try and control your impulses.'

'Sorry,' said Ella.

'Ach, have you forgotten how impulsive you were at that age?' Grizzly called from the couch.

A look of delight came over Fiona. 'What did she do?'

'Thank you, Mother,' said Morag. 'I don't need your input.'

'Well, you can't get away with forgetting as long as I'm here!' She cackled. 'There was this one time,' she said, looking at Fiona and ignoring Morag's frown, 'your ma was helping your grandad with the lambing. It was raining something wicked, really hossing down, and Grandad must have left the brakes off his quad bike — it was a new-fangled thing back then, and he never got used to it, much preferred horses — and it started to roll down the hill. Well, your ma saw this happening when Grandad was busy helping a sheep deliver, but instead of telling him, she just took off after it. Picture her, sloshing through all that mud, slub-slab, in her giant oversized oilskin raincoat and gumboots. She jumped on that bike and rode it all the way down the hill in the rain, not knowing how to stop it. She crashed into a fence at the bottom. It was a miracle she wasn't killed. But she got up and walked away, fine as you like. Something was looking out for her that day, I can tell ye.'

Morag rolled her eyes. 'It wasn't a hill, Ma, it was a gentle slope. It bumped into the fence, it didn't crash.'

'Took the fence clean out.' Grizzly laughed.

'Stop trying to change the subject.'

'Oh aye, don't get me started on when you were a teenager and the trouble you got into.'

'Okay they get it!'

Ella and Fiona were laughing now, imagining their sensible mother tearing off into the night, kicking up a cloud of mischief.

'That's what the women-folk in this family are like, hen, and there's no getting away from it. We're impulsive, rough and rabble-rousers.'

Ella stood up straighter.

'Not me,' said Fiona.

'You're your own person, it's true, love,' said Grizzly. 'You have to dree your own weird.'

Snuggled up in her hooded dressing gown, Fiona's white, fluffy hair was beginning to dry already. She was pale everywhere — pale skin, pale hair. Even her eyebrows were white. Ella, in contrast, had dark brown hair, almost black. Both Grizzly and Morag had black hair before it turned grey: Grizzly's when she was still a young woman, after she arrived in New Zealand; Morag's not long ago, after their dad disappeared six years ago.

'But where's your sense of adventure, Fifi?' said Ella.

Fiona studied her small white hands. 'Packed its bags and gone to have adventures without me.'

Even Morag laughed, but then she stiffened. 'I don't have time for this.' She grabbed the thermos and put it in her backpack.

Ella climbed up to where Fiona sat on the stairs and put her arm around her. 'I should stay with you,' she said.

'No.' Fiona's little face was determined. 'You should go. I need you to go. Please.'

'Ach, let her go and look for her friend,' said Grizzly. 'We'll be fine here. I can ring you if I need you.'

Ella looked at her mum, who looked back and rolled her eyes.

'All right, fine. Get your warmest coat. Hat, gloves.'

'Now, bairn.' Grizzly looked up at Fiona. 'I don't want to go traipsing up and down those stairs, so how's about you come and snuggle up with me in my bed, and I'll tell you some good Scottish folk tales — happy ones, don't give me that look. I know I normally like scaring you witless but I promise I'll be kind.'

Fiona was grinning now, and she stood up and jumped down each of the steps. Cuddling up in bed with Grizzly was the best thing that could happen to a girl, and Ella realised with a pang that she hadn't done it for a long time.

3

Shirr: a ruffle on the surface of water

A crowd of cars and SUVs was parked in the dark paddock by the Underhills' house. The beams of torches scraped the moist air. Ella's gumboots made a drumming, crunching sound on the driveway as they approached the crowd. A lot of adults stood around, and there was an expectant air, like a Guy Fawkes party waiting for a fireworks display. She spotted blonde twins Sigrid and Thomasin from school and gave them a shy wave, but they looked straight through her.

Ella could feel inside her skin that no good had come to Josh Underhill, and it might be her fault. 'No,' she said

16

to herself, trying to shake the feeling off; it wouldn't do anybody any good after all.

Josh's mother Susan was talking to Chris, the policeman. Nearby, two flaming torches spattered flickering shadows and orange light across their faces. Susan's jaw was tight, her mouth a grim line as she listened. Josh's father was a mountain behind her, his hands on her shoulders. Ella had first seen Ross Underhill when he had bundled his huge, angry body into his Land Rover outside their house while Grizzly and Morag stood, arms crossed and feet planted, in the doorway. Josh had been a shadow in the passenger seat, but he turned at the last minute and caught Ella's eye through the back window, a simmering reflection of his father.

Now, hovering nearby, a boy about her own age caught her attention. She'd never seen him before; he didn't go to her school. Perhaps he was older than he looked. He wore a jacket and pants that were too big for him and a woollen beanie pulled down over his ears, with tufts of unruly dark hair peeking out. He had that look of teenage boys who have grown too quickly — all mouth and nose and thick black eyebrows in a long narrow face. He caught her gaze and held it, until she looked away, embarrassed. There was something fiery in his eyes, probably the reflection of all the torchlight. As Susan

17

and her husband wandered off, it occurred to Ella that he'd been eavesdropping.

At last, Chris called the crowd to attention.

'Right, everyone! As you know, young Josh has gone missing. He's got off the school bus at about 3.30 p.m. at the end of his driveway, but he hasn't come home. Susan and Ross say he does like to go wandering — down to the lake sometimes — but we're not going to think the worst. Let's all spread out in a radius from here, and we'll keep ringing around, in the hope he's been picked up by a friendly neighbour and is having a cup of tea somewhere and just forgotten to call his mum.

'Pay careful attention to any ditches or drops. I want some of you to head up the Ben in case he's had a fall and can't walk. Just the lower slope — I can't imagine he'd go further than that and we don't want to be sending out search parties to find the search parties in the dark.'

Soon they set out walking, sweeping torches back and forth, fanning out across the countryside. Every now and then someone called out 'Joshua!' and it was answered by another further away, and another, until *Josh-u-a* echoed across the land. If he hadn't realised people were looking for him, thought Ella, he surely must know now. Where was he?

Ella and Morag were in the group heading to the lake

edge. If not for the worry about Josh, Ella could almost have imagined they were at one of the midwinter solstice parties her family used to host each year, with bonfires, and steaming cups of hot chocolate, and Dad playing his fiddle, or looming out of the shadows on his horse, with deer antlers on his head like Herne the Hunter, bellowing. Ella was only small, but she had memories of being terrified and loving it, a shotgun scatter of children running away screaming, much to the annoyance of some of the parents.

The night was getting colder. The wind had died away, but their breath made patterns in the darkness and the full blanket of stars looked down. As they approached the lake, Ella felt the air thicken — that was the only way she could think to describe it. She thought of her father, gone from its shore six years ago, never to be seen again. She thought of her grandfather, whose boat had been found drifting back to the beach. They said the lake was so deep nobody had ever been able to dive to the bottom, though many had tried. It was like a deep valley under there, with cliffs and caves and who knows what hiding within. Ella had always been fascinated by stories of the Loch Ness monster, and of the stories of taniwha, creatures who occupied bodies of water up and down the country, guardians of the lakes and the rivers.

A track scalloped around the lake's shoreline. Ella shivered inside her coat. The water was dark, with a slight wind ruffling its surface. White caps, like white horses, shirred and flashed in the starlight and in the flicker of torches. *Go jump in the lake, Josh Underhill.* Ella felt the lake's power then, the power of the secrets it held, and whether he was in there or had disappeared some other way, she was filled suddenly with a crashing dread. A small whimper escaped her.

'Hey,' said her mother. 'Are you okay, love?' She placed a reassuring hand on her daughter's shoulder blade and rubbed. 'He'll turn up, he has to.' But her voice didn't sound convincing.

'Hi there.' Someone fell into step beside Ella. It was the boy with the woollen hat.

'Hi,' said Ella. She wasn't used to people stopping and talking to her. He definitely wasn't from around here.

Morag merely glanced at him, no doubt assuming Ella knew him from school.

'Do you think they'll find him?' His soft voice surprised her — a low burr, like Grizzly. Scottish.

'I hope so,' she said. She did hope so, didn't she? Yes, of course she did.

'Did you know him?' he asked.

'A bit,' she said. The silence at the end became

20

awkward as he waited for her to go on.

'But you didn't like him much,' he said. 'Aye, I can tell.' He laughed.

Ella looked at Morag, but she was intent on shining her torch under bushes by the side of the track and wasn't listening.

'That's got nothing to do with it,' she said.

'All right now, you don't have to tell me.' He chuckled again and put his hands in his pockets. He began whistling a low tune, so quietly Ella couldn't make it out. He was behaving as if he was out for a Sunday stroll, not searching for a missing boy. He had no torch with him and no worry on his shoulders.

'Where did you come from, anyway?' she asked. Her mouth felt petulant. She couldn't help it. She didn't like the way he had used the past tense when speaking about Josh.

'Oh, I'm just here for a wee visit.'

'From Scotland?'

'Aye, something like that,' he said. He smiled at her, and her annoyance lifted somewhat. It was impish, cheeky. *Cheeky wee tyke*, Grizzly would have called him.

'My nan's from Scotland,' she said.

'Is that right?' he said, but it was insincere, as if he already knew, or as if he wasn't interested in the slightest.

'What's your name?' he asked.

She told him. He repeated it back to her. 'Ella. *Ella.*' It sounded musical in his mouth, like a song. 'Right, Ella. I'm away. See you soon.' And with that, he fell back into the shadows and was gone. Ella shone her torch after him, but she'd lost him.

'Who was that?' said Morag. 'He seemed friendly.' There was hope in her voice, which made Ella's heart ache just a little bit.

'I don't know,' said Ella. 'I've never seen him before. He's Scottish.'

'Oh, we should tell Grizzly,' said Morag. 'She might like to meet his family, especially if they're new around here.'

'Yeah,' said Ella. New was better.

THEY SEARCHED FOR an hour, with no sign of Josh. No shouts in the distance, no *found him!* or *over here!* The wind had picked up again and Ella hoped that Josh was sheltering somewhere. And that he had a coat.

Her feet ached with the cold and the walking. She didn't complain, but her steps became slower, sluggish, and her mother took one look at her and said, 'Look at you, you're dead on your feet. We need to call it a night.' She called to another mother. 'I have to get this one home. Call me if you hear anything.' There was an indistinct reply, and then they were trudging back to the car.

They didn't have far to drive, but by the time they got home, Ella had nodded off and her mother was shaking her to take her inside, then helping her out of her clothes so she could collapse into bed.

4

Undersong: the sounds of a landscape
Roke: thick mist that rises from
damp ground like smoke

Ella lay tangled in her duvet, limbs stuck in all directions like they were trying to crawl off to different corners of the room. First day of the spring holidays and still she had to get up early to help Morag with the horses — after such an exhausting night, too.

Where was Josh Underhill?

People talked about how sad it was that Ella and Fiona had lost their father. *Lost*. As in *misplaced*. How do you misplace something as big as a father? It wasn't like when she lost her library book, or the million little things she could never find before school — her shoes, her hat, her jacket, her homework — even though she was sure she'd left them right where they should be. Saying they had lost him made it sound as though it was their fault. It made Ella realise, more than ever, how words matter. Choose them carefully. Maybe Dad *was* misplaced, that was all, though it wasn't through her and her sister's carelessness. And if that was so, then mightn't they find him one day, behind the sofa, where she'd finally found her shoes yesterday morning?

Maybe Josh was just temporarily misplaced.

She sighed and regrouped her arms and legs, tripping over last night's boots and coat as she dragged herself to the window.

It was still dark outside, with just a wash of light at the horizon. She could sense rather than see the horses — black shapes in the fog. She liked to think that she and Magpie had a special connection, that they could read each other — certainly Magpie had given her more love and friendship than any of the kids at school. Magpie had come into her life at just the right time, when worry and grief from losing her father had threatened to overwhelm her as it had her mother; when Grizzly became obsessed and fell out with the town over a conservation issue. With Magpie to take her attention, Ella could believe that her father was not really gone.

THE MIRACLE FILLY THEY called her. Olive, the albino mare, who was as pale as milk, was getting fatter by the day. The vet was called and they discovered she was with foal. Morag was baffled. There were no stallions for miles, and the horses were kept safe behind fences or in the stable. When Olive finally lay down, huffing, and the shiny package slipped out from under her tail, they joked that a mystery horse had flown in on wings, or that the faeries had got to her. An immaculate conception.

Olive licked the parcel clean, and the creature unfolded itself like a spider, wobbled on spindly legs. She was white, with black splotches — or was it black with white splotches? The black was so deep it was iridescent, like the feathers of a raven, sometimes flashing green in the sunlight. She was like the snow thawing in patches on the sides of the Ben. They called her Magpie, after the black and white birds that roamed the landscape, that came to watch her be born, jostling each other for a view. The strangest thing about her, though, was her ears. Instead of being strong and long, like her mother's, they were small and delicate, like petals.

Ella was eight when Magpie was born, and in love with her straight away. Beglamoured, Grizzly said, and Magpie with her. The filly followed Ella around the field, but wouldn't let anyone else get near her. When the vet checked her, Ella was the only one who could calm her, standing at her head and murmuring into her cockle-shell ears.

Three years later, when it came time to break her in, Magpie wouldn't tolerate even the saddle pad on her back unless Ella was with her, and as Morag lunged her, she kicked and squealed at the end of the long rein rather than move in a steady circle. Morag almost gave up in frustration until Ella convinced her to let her try.

'Look at you,' said Morag. 'You're a natural.'

But when they tried to put a bit between her teeth to fit her bridle, Magpie was having none of it. She threw her head up and screeched, her eyes wide cauldrons. Afterwards, Ella found blisters on the corners of her pony's mouth.

'That's strange,' said Morag. 'She must have had some kind of allergic reaction to the metal.' They waited until it had healed and tried again with a rubber bit, which Magpie accepted much more readily, but the sores reappeared. Morag grudgingly bought her a bitless bridle, and within a couple of weeks Ella was riding her, trotting in a circle around the small outdoor arena.

'It's almost as if it was made for her,' said Morag in wonder. 'I think you've even got more control, Ellie — she's really listening to you.'

The one time Morag tried to ride her, Magpie shied and bucked and threw her off. She wasn't hurt, but she did threaten to send the pony away.

'We can't have horses that can't be ridden here,' she said. 'They cost money to keep. It's not worth it.'

'But I can ride her. She can be my pony. I'll do everything to look after her. I'll help out and earn pocket money which you can keep.'

Morag relented, and Magpie tolerated having Ella throw her arms around her neck and bury her face in her mane, crying tears of relief.

'IT'S GOING TO be a fine day,' said Morag, when Ella arrived downstairs for her breakfast. 'But cold at first with that fog. Make sure you get your jacket on. Here. Eat up quick. We've got lots to do.' She put a bowl of steaming porridge in front of Ella, who poured milk and a sprinkle of brown sugar on top.

'Did they find him?' Ella's voice felt small, pale.

'No, love. I'm sorry.' Morag busied herself at the sink, her back to Ella and Fiona, who was already at the table eating cornflakes. There was a stiffness in her shoulders, and she let out a great sigh. 'I can't imagine what they must be going through, Susan and Ross.' She was barely

28

audible over the sound of the running tap. Because of course she could imagine. Her own husband had never been found. Ella knew they were all thinking about him.

'Morning!' Grizzly's nurse Rita was at the doorway, wiping her feet and pulling off her hat, exposing short frizzy red hair. She grabbed Ella as she came in and hugged her, radiating cold from the outside air that had become trapped inside her coat.

'You'll be feeling worried about Josh Underhill, sweetheart,' she said, her red-cheeked face crinkled in concern. 'Is he a friend of yours?' She cupped Ella's jaw, but Ella dropped her eyes and shrugged, blushing, before escaping out the door.

Outside, Ella patted her pockets as she always did to make sure she had everything. The bulge in one pocket of her riding jacket was the carrot pieces, and her gloves were in the other. She had Morag's old phone, too, for emergencies. It wasn't much use for anything else — it didn't even take pictures.

She grabbed three halters from the tack room and opened the gate to the home paddock. A magpie's song cut through the still, damp air, musical and demanding. The birds really made a racket at this time of the morning; they often woke Ella before her alarm went off.

Magpie whickered long and loud across the sea of

mist that was just beginning to thin on the ground. Ella shifted the halters on her arm and readied the carrot pieces. Magpie walked towards her, little ears pricked, stepping high, but Joey the bay gelding and Duke the skewbald cob ignored her, cropping grass and pretending they weren't looking at her out of the corner of their eyes.

Fiona's black Shetland pony came high-stepping across the paddock, showing off like a Tennessee Walking Horse, even though he was tiny — his back only came up to Ella's stomach. His thick mane stood up in tufts, shot through with dried mud.

'Get away, Peedie, you cheeky wee tyke,' said Ella, pushing him with an elbow against his shaggy neck. Ella didn't have enough carrots to feed him too, and he trotted off again in disgust.

The horses all had their covers on, rugged up against the cold. This was the job Ella was supposed to have helped Morag with after school — no wonder her mother had been grumpy when she came in.

'Good girl, Maggie,' she said as she slipped the halter over Magpie's nose and quickly did up the buckle. She draped the lead rope across the pony's neck; she knew she wouldn't go anywhere.

The other two horses had drifted away from her like flotsam on the surface of the lake. At least they hadn't taken off for the hill as some of the horses liked to do, making their humans chase them all over the High Country. She patted Duke's neck. He was like a patch-work toy, with a chestnut head and neck, and a white patch that looked like Australia on his side. He accepted the carrot, but tossed his head when she tried to put the halter on. 'Stand up!' she said in her growliest voice, which she had learnt from her mother. Duke shifted from hoof to hoof, but stayed still long enough for Ella to put it on.

Joey put his ears back at first, but softened when he smelled the carrot. Ella patted his nose and traced the line of the interrupted stripe that ran down his face like two fingers, tips reaching for each other. He nudged her arm with thanks. Soon Ella had all three horses in hand and started leading them back to the stable area where their hay was waiting.

Her mind wandered to last night: the cold, the torches, the night sounds and the rustling; the gentle lap of the lake and glimpse of white ruffles on its surface. The huge, indifferent sky, awash with stars. The strange Scottish boy. She'd given him her name, but she didn't know his.

She'd never been down by the lake so late, and all night long she'd had strange dreams of searching for her father, walking along the edge of the water, calling for him. Eventually she had found a camping chair and fishing rod, and as she'd called again, a great groaning came from the black lake. She'd woken up, hot, in the dark morning.

Now, one of the ropes jerked out of her hand. She cried out, startled and with a wash of shame — Morag had taught her to be vigilant around the horses, especially leading three at once, and always to concentrate. The other two ropes were taut, but all three horses stood their ground, stiff-legged, heads high. Listening.

Joey let out a high whinny and suddenly backed away. Ella lost that rope too, and tightened her grip on Magpie, moving closer to her head. There was no doubt: something had spooked the horses. Joey and the usually dependable Duke trembled, their eyes wide.

Then she heard it. An unearthly cry, part horse, part screeching bird. And hoofbeats, winnowing towards them. Beyond the paddock, towards the lake. Out of the mist, a huge dark shape emerged like a spreading pool of ink. A black horse, an apparition, moved in a lazy canter along the far fenceline of the paddock. All four of them, girl and horses, held their breaths as if in a spell, and watched it swirl through the roke and come to a stop. Head held high, it turned to face them and snorted. There were no other sounds in the landscape. Even the undersong — the constant sounds of the land, of trilling birds, sheep, distant dogs and car engines, buzzing insects, the singing of the wind through grass and wire fences — died away.

The mist rising from the ground clambered thickly at the animal's legs, creating the illusion that it was standing on a cloud in a stormy sky. The horse pawed the ground, once, twice, three times. Then it wheeled and took off again, back into the fog, its pounding hooves fading to nothing.

Ella found she had been gripping Magpie's rope hard. The ropes of the other two horses trailed on the ground. Duke and Joey had stopped trembling, and were now casually cropping grass as if nothing strange had happened. But Ella's heart was beating hard in her chest. Magpie, too, was still tetchy, dancing on her feet. Her neck felt hot and damp as it did when she'd been galloping on a summer's day, and a brief lick of steam rose from her.

'Well, that was unexpected!' Ella said. 'You okay, Maggie?' She gave her pony a hearty clap on her filthy neck, as if by acting casual Magpie would forget what had happened, as Duke and Joey seemed to have.

* * *

33

magpie feather one
magpie feather two
a piece of smooth blue glass I found on the shore of the lake
a frog bone from my father's collection, fragile and round
a dried-up bumblebee, curled like a flower
a bird claw, and beside it
a tiny bird skull, picked clean and smooth
one feather sharp and brown, from a pheasant
my new magpie feather, white with a black tip

Fiona laid her latest treasures out on the windowsill in order, and touched each one, singing, low and sweet, a tune that Grizzly had taught her. She had seen the black horse too, but she knew her mother hadn't because she could hear her downstairs, talking to Rita and Grizzly, making sure they were set up for the day.

She selected the circular bone, a magpie feather and an unusual rock with a hole in it that she'd found by the stone circle at the back of the house. A *hagstone*, Grizzly had called it — good luck. There was also a dried rowan sprig, the berries shrivelled and black, no hint of their plump redness. Grizzly called that *witch wiggin*, for keeping the evil spirits at bay. She'd planted a rowan tree by the front gate of the house a long time ago, and it had grown and reached for the sky. The birds had fed on the fat jewels and carried the seeds all over the paddocks and down to the lake.

Fiona tied them all together with string, singing all the while. She needed something else. Under her bed was a box. She knelt down and slid it out, sneezing once as a dust bunny came out with it. Inside the box, two of her baby teeth lay wrapped in tissue. She had already buried the first four in the stone circle — one for her, one for Ella, one for Morag and one for Grizzly — but she knew that Grizzly couldn't be protected from what came from inside her, and that was okay. She could keep them safe from other outside forces. She had already placed one of her talismans at the end of the driveway, hanging it from the letterbox where it twisted and spun in the wind.

Her father had collected treasure. Not diamonds and gold and rubies like a pirate's treasure. His had come from the natural world, like a tiny bird's nest with little speckled blue eggs in it. He had a glass-fronted cabinet in his office he called his 'cabinet of curiosities'.

But the cabinet no longer held treasure. Instead it held books and boxes of files for Morag's horse-trekking business. Their mother had thrown most of the cabinet's contents away, but Fiona had managed to rescue the nest and a few other treasures, and now she collected her own. As she daundered through the countryside, keeping her eyes sharp, she imagined she felt her father's hand in hers. Would he have been able to answer the questions she had as they walked, the ones nobody else was able to?

Like, *what if your emotions were separate from your body? What would they look like?* And, *why do you have to look at people when they talk to you, when it's your ears that hear them, not your eyes?*

She knew so little about him. Did she take after him? Were these the kinds of questions that he asked of the universe too? She longed to hear him play his violin, which now sat in the corner of Morag's room, gathering dust. Fiona would like to play it one day, but Morag said she had to wait until she was older and could be more careful. Ella didn't show any interest in it.

She pushed the baby teeth aside to get to the real prize. She lifted it from the box and slid her fingers over its bony smoothness: a yellowed tooth as long as her hand was wide. She tested the end — still sharp and strong enough to break the bones of your wrist if applied with force. She would give this one back to the earth, among the stones. It would keep them all safe. She slid the box back under her bed, gathered her fresh talisman, and headed for the door.

5

Glumfie: moody; grumpy
Yirdit: muddy; from the earth
Liminal: the boundary between two worlds

'There you are,' said Morag as Ella and the horses clopped into the stable yard. She grabbed Duke and Joey and led them to their spots along the fence, where she tied their ropes through the twine that was looped through metal rings. Piles of hay were spaced out on the ground nearby.

'Mōrena!' It was Hana, the young woman who worked for Morag as a riding instructor and guide. She'd pulled up in her neat little hatchback and was heading straight inside the tack room to get three more halters. 'Who are we getting today?' she asked as she emerged.

'Rocky, Jubilee, Storm and Zippy, I think,' said Morag. 'We've got a bunch of beginners, down from up north. I'll stay behind, so we can leave Olive and you can take Sir Ed. I'm going to give Fiona her riding lesson.'

'Did you see the horse?' called Ella, and she was surprised to hear her voice sounded breathless, as though she'd been running.

'Which horse?'

'A black one. It was huge. A stallion, I think. It spooked our horses.' She saw it again in her mind. The shape of it, the blackness, like it had sucked all of the light out of the day.

'I don't know any stallions around here. Was it Ted's mare Angel? Maybe she's got out. We should call him.'

Ella shook her head. 'No, it wasn't Angel. This horse was much blacker. And much bigger. I know what I saw.'

'Yeah, okay, love,' said her mother as she pushed her arm through a couple of halters to carry them over her shoulder. 'I'm not doubting you. Did you see anything, Hana, as you were driving in?'

'Nope.' Hana ran her flat palm back and forth over her short, spiky black hair that was bleached on the tips. She wore dark blue jodhpurs and long riding boots, with a puffer jacket. She guided most of the treks; she wasn't afraid to chat with strangers and tell them stories about the landscape they were trekking through. Her family had been here for generations, and their stories were embedded in the land, her tūpuna — her Ngāi Tahu ancestors — embodied in the mountains and lakes.

Ella adored her and never forgot how patient she was when teaching her to ride, always quick with a kind word or a riding tip. It was Hana who taught her to bring Magpie to a halt by sitting up straight in the saddle and redistributing her weight, and she never barked at Ella, or told her off for not listening when her mind wandered. She'd just bring her back with a gentle word and repeat the instructions, demonstrating visually so Ella could understand better.

Morag was not so patient with beginners, and often lost her temper when she thought the horses were being mistreated in any small way that was obvious only to herself. She was not so patient with Ella either, but Ella couldn't help it — as soon as Morag started explaining something in great detail, Ella's mind wandered off, even if she concentrated really hard on watching her mother's lips move. It had resulted in quite a few tears and one or other of them storming off in frustration.

Hana and Morag set out to catch the remaining horses, and left Ella to take off the covers and groom the other three. She started on Magpie, stopping to stroke her face and her velvet chin, the few coarse hairs like tussock. Magpie stood placidly and closed her eyes sleepily, no longer alert to the other humans, who made her edgy, stroppy even.

'*Glumfie*, aren't you,' said Ella, ruffling Magpie's fore-lock, trying out the new word she'd found in the pocket of her riding jacket. Grizzly must have put it there when they were out last night. 'Well, let's get you clean, since nobody else can get near you.' Actually, she thought, *glumfie* was probably too soft a word for Magpie and her mercurial nature. *Devilish* was more apt.

Ella worked hard and fast with a stiff-bristled dandy brush, flicking off the caked-on dirt. Then she grabbed a body brush to polish her. The sun was breaking through the last of the mist, and it shone on the liquorice patches that were emerging now, glossy, from the dust.

She tutted. 'What have you been doing out there? Finding all the mud you can roll in?' The white patch in Magpie's mane was also stained green with poo, which after all was mostly made of grass, and had a tangled knot in it. As Ella worked on it with a comb she realised she hadn't brushed her own hair in days. She spent more time grooming Magpie than she did herself.

Fiona appeared at the other end of the yard, brushing her hands down her front. They were caked in dirt as though she'd been playing in the mud, and now her yellow coat was too.

'Hello, *yirdit wee gussie!*' called Ella. That was what Grizzly used to call them when they tumbled inside — happy, dirty little pigs. 'Decided to join us? Grab a brush, please — start with Duke.'

Fiona nodded. Duke loved kids. In the summer they doubled on him bareback and slid off his rear. Despite his heft, Morag trusted him completely with beginners.

By the time Morag and Hana were back with the other five horses, Magpie was brushed and her hooves cleaned. Ella was now finishing off Joey, while Fiona was still working on Duke. For all her timidity she was a natural around horses. She was tiny but had no trouble enticing Duke to lift his heavy feet while she scraped at the stones inside. She worked slowly and methodically, chatting to the gelding as she went, playing her favourite game: Imagine.

Imagine a secret society, just for shushing birds
Imagine surfing with a sloth on your back
Imagine if you were big enough to have your own
*   atmosphere*
Imagine if sheep had eyes in their tails but we didn't know
*   because we cut them off*

Duke just munched his hay, listening.

Ella started on Sir Edmund Hillary, Morag's huge dun, removing his cover and giving him a vigorous brushing — the parts she could reach on tip-toes.

'Move back, you big oaf,' she said as Sir Ed's imposing bulk, all seventeen hands, pressed against her. 'Oof, okay, teddy bear.' She relented and paused what she was doing to give him the cuddle he was seeking.

THEY WORKED QUICKLY, grooming the remaining horses, fitting them with their saddles and bridles, but leaving their halters on so they could stay tethered. Then Morag and Fiona went to catch Peedie, Fiona's Shetland pony, for her lesson.

Morag was right — it had turned into a beautiful morning. Just before ten o'clock two rental cars pulled up. The occupants looked nervous as they got out.

'Kia ora!' called Hana. Because Morag's face often looked strained and grumpy, it was Hana's job to greet the customers, take their money, and have them sign a health and safety contract which said that they were riding at their own risk and would comply with all the rules — wearing a helmet at all times, following instructions.

It turned out that a couple of the riders were experienced, but the rest were beginners, so Hana gave them a demonstration on how to mount the horses off a mounting block. One of the experienced riders insisted on mounting from the ground, but Morag, hovering around while Fiona groomed Peedie, put a stop to that, saying she didn't need the extra strain on her tack thank you very much and could they do as they had been asked.

Soon the riders were on their horses, two men, one heavy and one wiry, three women and one boy who looked to be about twelve. The boy was on Zippy, the docile dappled grey they always used for beginners. He looked elated to be up there, and kept stroking Zippy's mane.

'Give him a scritch on his withers,' said Ella, showing him as she and Morag went along the line to make sure everyone was holding their reins properly and not pulling on the horses' mouths. 'He loves it.'

'Does he like apples?' asked the boy.

'Only green ones,' said Morag. 'If you feel yourself slipping or falling back, hold the saddle or his mane, don't jerk on his reins or you'll hurt his mouth.' She smiled kindly at the boy, who was eager to please. It was the ones who thought they knew better that Morag got cross with.

Hana mounted Sir Ed and took the lead; Ella, on Magpie, brought up the rear as they all filed down the driveway towards the bridle path. It was slow going with beginners, and Ella got bored easily. She wanted nothing more than to break away and go for a canter across the rolling paddock. But as long as Morag wanted to stay behind and look after Fiona, it was her job to keep to the back and make sure the horses didn't stop to crop grass or misbehave. From up high she watched Duke's chestnut tail swish back and forth over his chunky hocks, and Magpie's head bob around, taking in the sights.

It was peaceful, with the steady clop of the horses and the creak of the saddle beneath her. She moved her seat perfectly in tune with the rhythm of Magpie's walk, as though she and her pony were one. The day felt full of possibility but utterly predictable at the same time.

She thought of the boy she'd met, and found herself hoping she'd see him again. Even though he'd annoyed her a bit, she remembered his cheeky smile.

Maybe he could be the friend for the holidays she'd wished for? She'd always wanted someone to go riding with, to have adventures with, like in the endless pony books she'd gobbled when she was younger. She idly thought that maybe they would find Josh. Become heroes. She'd ask Morag to help her find out where the boy lived — she'd seemed keen on him too.

Magpie blew a raspberry that brought her attention back to the ride. Out the gate they went, and across the road to the track that led over the Kupa farm. It was a steep gradient up the side of the Ben, which loomed over them with its grey hide scarred with old landslides. Ella always felt it watching her: in the morning when she woke up and it was cast in shadow; in the afternoon as she walked home from the school bus; as she rode down to the lake, feeling its eyes resting on her shoulders; and in the grimmelings, when it grew black and silent, draining all the light from the indigo evening sky. At night she couldn't see it, except for its outline against the swipe of stars in the sky, but on clouded nights, when the stars were swallowed in the grey, she knew it was there, could feel it pressing down onto the earth.

Ella was glad she'd worn her gloves. An icy breeze was coming off the lake, which they could now see from the track. The riders were turning in their saddles, chattering excitedly about the view: the brown tussocky grass that gave the landscape its unique golden colour; the sparse trees groomed into bent-over shapes by the insistent wind; and, rising out of it all, the lake. On clear days it glowed turquoise, a creamy blue caused by the glaciers at the headwaters in the snowy mountains which circled the Basin.

'Leaning back slightly now!' called Hana as they started heading down the hill, and Ella took her cue to echo it from the back. Magpie's strange ears twitched at the sound of her voice.

The heavier man ahead of her grunted as solid Duke stumbled.

'You're fine, mister!' she called. 'Duke won't fall. He knows what he's doing.' *Just don't get him to trot while he's facing home*, she thought, *or he'll gallop the whole way.*

'Yes, I *am* fine,' the man muttered. Ella imagined that he had been dragged along on this expedition by his horsey wife, who was chatting up the front with Hana.

Facing south now, the breeze chilled their faces. Farmer Kupa's sheep stopped grazing the meagre grass to snap their heads up and watch them pass. Some pretended to startle, and skipped a few steps away, before shrugging and going back to their foraging. One or two lambs hid behind their mothers, and Ella found herself hoping there'd be no more cold snaps — it was supposed to be spring, but winter held on deep in the ground.

They reached the shore of the lake and turned east on the track that wove around the shore.

Ella gazed out at the water. As always there was a

large patch, a smooth mirror, amid its ruffled surface. The keld, they called it — one of the words that Grizzly had collected — which Ella always imagined as a witch's cauldron: a thin, liminal place, where magic happened, because no matter how choppy the lake's surface was, that spot stayed as still as you like.

It was from this shore that Ella's father, Will, had disappeared.

Ella heard a shout come from the front of the line, followed by groans.

'That's disgusting!' someone called. The line came to a halt.

Ella stood in her stirrups to try to see what was going on. The first few horses were standing side by side now, and the riders were looking at something in the grass by the track. Rocky was dancing, tossing his head, and looked like he was ready to turn and run for home, so Ella urged Magpie into a trot and moved up the line to see what the commotion was about. Rocky's rider was saying 'whoa, whoa!' and tugging at the reins, making the horse even more agitated. She was white in the face.

'Easy, Rocky,' said Ella in a soothing voice. 'There's the good horse. You're okay now.'

At the sound of her voice, and sensing Magpie's presence, Rocky calmed down.

'Thanks,' said the woman. 'I was worried he was going to bolt. My worst nightmare.' Her hands were shaking as much as her voice. 'That sheep must have freaked him out.'

'Which sheep?' said Ella, then she saw what everyone was looking at. One of Farmer Kupa's sheep lay beside the track. What was left of it. Its head had been removed, and blood crisscrossed its body.

Ella's stomach clenched. She tightened her grip on the reins as Magpie let out a disturbed rumble. The pony lifted her nose and sniffed at the wind, turning her head this way and that as if trying to spot who might have done this.

'What's happened, Hana?' she called. 'Who would do something like that?'

Hana was grim-mouthed. She stood up in her stirrups and shaded her eyes.

'There's another one over there, poor things.'

She pointed over the fence into the next paddock. A huddle of sheep stood shivering nearby, staring wild-eyed. Traumatised.

By now the rest of the riders had come up. Ella knew Morag would be furious if she saw the way they'd clustered together, bumping their horses against each other: they were supposed to stay in single file at all times for safety. But Hana seemed not to notice, and Ella didn't say anything; she was only a kid after all and who would listen to her? Not the grumpy man on Duke, that was for sure.

Instead, she looked for clues. No smashed fences that she could see, no animal prints or footprints on the trail, only hoofprints, likely from their own eight horses. But by the track, where Magpie stood, broken shrubs on both sides, and flattened grass. A channel leading from the paddock, where the sheep were, to the shore of the lake. She stood up in her stirrups for a better look and, yes, there it was. Two lines in the sand, a smear of blood on a log. Drag marks, into the lake.

6

Blirt: a gust of wind and rain;
a fit of crying

After they had watered the horses, given them some hay and left them tethered in the yard, Morag had lunch ready in the barn by the stables. Fiona joined them, her feet swinging from the too-big chair. The barn was stacked with hay bales, which kept it cosy and warm against the chill outside. The blue sky was disappearing now, an inky cloud rolling across it.

'Is that rain?' said Morag, frowning at the cloud. 'It's not forecast.'

Nobody answered. The atmosphere was creepy, the barn too dark.

Ella took a piece of bread and squashed some ham and cheese into it. 'What about the sheep?' Her voice came out as a whisper.

Morag's face ruffled with concern. 'Oh, my darling, I'm sorry you had to see that. It must have been scary. I would have jumped out of my skin.' She wouldn't have. She was only saying it to make Ella feel better.

Ella just nodded and took a bite of her sandwich. The image of the headless sheep came to her, the drag marks into the lake.

'It was pretty grim,' said Hana. 'I've seen dead sheep before, but this was something else.'

'Poor sheep,' said Fiona.

'Someone's going to pay for that damage,' said Morag. 'And when they find the dog, it'll be put down. We can't have sheep killers roaming free. I wonder if it was some-one's city dog let loose?'

Ella stopped chewing and looked at Hana, who nodded.

'A dog?' she said. 'You think it was a dog?'

'What else could it have been?'

'One of them had its head ripped clean off!'

'Ella!' hissed Morag, and looked sideways at Fiona, who had stopped swinging her legs and was staring at Ella in horror.

'Is it true, Mum?' she whispered. 'Did the sheep have no head? What if it had a lamb?' Her pale face reddened and her cheeks puffed. Her eyes filled with tears.

Morag reached over and patted her leg. 'Oh sweetheart, yes, I'm afraid it's true. But don't worry, Mr Kupa will make sure it doesn't happen again.'

Fiona squeezed her eyes shut and nodded. 'Mum,' she said. 'I don't think it was a dog. I think it was a wolf, come down off the Ben. The same wolf that took Josh Underhill.'

Imagine a wolf came down off the Ben and took Josh Underhill

A chill wind slipped into the barn. Dark clouds filled Ella's head.

'Why would you think it's a wolf?' said Hana, the first to speak.

'I just know it. Something with sharp teeth, and fiery, smoking eyes. Something wild and uncontainable.' She said it with no sense of foreboding in her voice, as if she was merely reciting a recipe for cake, though her face was still dwelling on the dead animals.

'Also,' she said. 'I found a tooth. A big, sharp tooth.'

Morag frowned and looked at Hana. 'A wild pig? A tusk?'

Hana shrugged but looked uncertain. Nobody said anything.

Outside, a blirt of sudden rain rattled the tin roof, then was gone again.

'Funny weather this,' said Morag, breaking the cold silence. 'And we don't have wolves in this country, poppet. Pigs, yes, but there aren't any around here. Josh will come home, I'm sure of it. Someone in town thought they saw him getting on the bus north this morning; he might have just run away from home. They'll find him.'

Fiona looked sceptical, and Ella wasn't so sure either. Their eyes met for a second — Ella's dark grey and Fiona's pale cloud eyes. An unspoken understanding moved between them. The lake had a way of playing tricks on people, making them see things they wanted to see. You live too long beside it and you come under its spell. But Ella shook the thought of Josh and whatever killed the sheep out of her head. She concentrated on picturing him, his bag slung over his shoulder, taking one last look at the town before he turned and boarded the bus to a new adventure.

ELLA WAS OUT with Magpie, drying her saddle after the brief shower, when something caught her eye. A figure stood in the horses' paddock, patting Olive the mare.

53

The world tilted, and Ella shuddered. Whoever it was saw her looking, raised a hand and began walking towards her.

It was the boy from the other night. He was dressed in the same oversized jacket and beanie pulled low on his forehead. For a moment Ella wondered if she'd summoned him just by thinking about him. How did he find her?

He laughed as he approached. Olive was following him, her head down, nose almost touching his legs.

'Your face,' he said.

'You gave me a fright,' she said, and put her hand on her chest where her heart was still knocking at the door to get out.

He stopped on the other side of the fence, well away from Magpie, who was eyeing him suspiciously. 'I know. I can hear your heart beating from here. That was some burst of weather we had, don't you think?'

They both looked up. The sky was blue again, as though the black cloud had never been there. Instead, small white clouds puffed across the horizon like a school of silver fish with somewhere important to be.

'Yeah,' said Ella. 'Unexpected.' She held up the towel as if he'd know what she'd been doing with it. He said nothing, so she casually draped it over the fencepost.

He came forward and raised a hand towards Magpie's nose. Magpie flattened her ears and clattered back a few steps to the end of her rope, trembling.

'Stand still, Maggie,' said Ella. 'It's only a boy, silly horse. She doesn't much like people, sorry. Unless they're on another horse, then she's fine. It's just the ones on the ground she doesn't trust.'

'Doesn't she now? Well, I suppose that's normal, I don't much like them myself. Nasty, horrible people.' And he laughed.

As if to show her filly up, Olive put her chin on the boy's shoulder and blew in his ear.

'Get off!' he said good-naturedly, and shrugged her away.

'You've made a friend, I see,' said Ella. They were standing there as if it was the most normal thing in the world to be talking like this. But Ella said what she was thinking. 'What are you doing here?'

'I'm just out for a walk. Hey, do you think I could go for a ride with you? If your pony doesn't like me on the ground, maybe she'd be all right with me on one of your other horses.' He stroked Olive's forelock, and she closed her eyes in bliss. Ella had never seen her so friendly.

'I don't even know your name!' said Ella.

The boy smiled his cheeky grin. 'It's Gus. Pleased to meet you.' He walked forward as if to shake her hand, but Magpie threw up her head and snorted, stopping him in his tracks.

'Can you ride?'

'Och aye, I know my way around a beastie.' He winked.

'You're like an old man, you know that?' said Ella, but she smiled. 'And sure, I'll ask my mum. Should be okay.'

'Thanks, Ella Ella.'

At the sound of her double name a warm wave washed through her belly. Company would be good. Hadn't she just been thinking about that? Solving crimes, finding treasure. That sort of thing?

'I hear they didn't find that boy last night,' said Gus. 'What do you suppose happened to him?'

'I don't know. Maybe we should go and have a look up in the old church.'

'Church?'

'Up over there.' She pointed. The building was a smudge against the distant hill.

'All right,' he said, but he looked doubtful.

She left him in the paddock and found Morag about to leave the barn.

'I don't see why not,' said Morag, pulling on her jacket. 'Nice for you to have a friend, if he's experienced. Is he?'

'He says so.'

'Let's find out, shall we.'

Morag smiled her most welcoming smile at Gus. It was slightly disarming — but Ella realised that she was putting on a show to not scare him away.

'Nice to meet you, Gus,' she said brightly. 'Let's choose you a horse, shall we?' All the horses were tethered again, ready for Hana to lead another ride.

'Can I ride this white one?' Gus asked, giving Olive a hearty clap on the neck. She nudged him in return.

'She's not normally so friendly,' said Morag. 'But no, she's a bit too fiery for you to ride.'

'I like fiery,' said Gus. 'I usually ride bareback.' He climbed over the fence into the yard where the trek horses stood. Olive crowded the gate hopefully as he went to open it.

'Easy there,' said Morag. 'I've said no.' Her mask had slipped a little, and Gus stopped, hearing it in her voice, though he didn't move away. 'Maybe another time, Gus, but we'll put you on Zippy to start with. He's grey, so nearly white. And I'm not letting you on bareback, so you can forget about that.'

'*Mum, no.*' Ella rolled her eyes. 'Not Zippy. We'd like to go faster than a crawl. What about Duke?'

'No, we need Duke for this afternoon's trek.' Morag

paused, turning the choices over in her mind. 'You can have Storm, but *no galloping*. Okay? He might have failed as a racehorse but he's still got the competitive spirit. You'll have no trouble controlling him as long as you don't go too fast. Got it, Ellie?'

'Of course,' she said, already planning the best paddock for a race.

She took Gus over to meet Storm and help get him ready. 'We call him Slightly Drizzly Afternoon,' she said. 'He's a thoroughbred but he doesn't really live up to his real name.'

Gus rode with confidence but he was awkward in the stirrups, as though he couldn't bear for his feet to be restrained. His boots were old and worn, and looked like they should be thrown away. As he rode, his toes pointed down and his elbows flapped, which made Ella laugh inside. His hands were gentle on the bright bay's mouth though, and Storm was happy to do as he was asked, almost as if he was reading Gus's mind.

They crossed through the horses' paddock and into the fields beyond. Sheep scattered when they came near.

'It's nice country around here,' said Gus. He was bumping in the saddle as Storm jogged along. 'It reminds me of Scotland. These bare hills, the rocks. The loch of course.'

'That's what my nan says. I think that's why she ended up here.'

'Oh, aye? Why'd she leave Scotland?'

'I'm not sure. She doesn't talk about it much.'

Grizzly had grown up by a Highland lake, a loch, very much like this one. She said she wouldn't be surprised if she could have dived down and down into its depths and resurfaced here on the other side of the world. But instead she had come by boat, a weeks-long journey across oceans, sickness heaving in her belly the whole way.

She had left Scotland and never been back, finding herself a husband and settling down in the place that reminded her most of home. She had hinted at a great sadness that forced her to leave, but she had never spoken of it, just said, 'My heart was too sore to stay, and it's sore when I think about it again.' Then she would turn away and change the subject.

When Ella asked Morag about it, her mother just said that Grizzly had told her she didn't have any family left, and to put it out of her mind. Morag got the distinct feeling she didn't want to be asked about it.

But Ella remembered how a few years ago, before Grizzly got sick, she had been walking down by the lake and had heard a low melody coming from the shore, near the keld. She'd hidden in a scrubby bush and peeped down at Grizzly, standing by the shore, singing a dark lament in her husky voice. She only recognised some words, but she knew she was singing in Scottish Gaelic, and she could tell that the song was sad and Grizzly was too. Ella assumed she was singing for her husband, taken by the lake all those years ago. She wanted to go down and hold her hand, to comfort her, but she knew better than to disturb her, and turned back before she was missed for too long from home.

Ella didn't say any of this to Gus. 'Did you ever go to Loch Ness?' she asked instead.

'Oh aye,' he said, smirking.

'Did you see the Loch Ness monster?'

'Sure,' he said.

'Liar.' Ella smiled.

'Scotland used to be full of all kinds of creatures. The faerie world is not as far away as you think. That's what we believe anyway.'

'Fiona thinks there's a wolf here. On the Ben.'

'Is that right. Why does she think that?'

'Some sheep were killed. Horrible. One of them had its head taken off.' Ella shuddered at the memory. 'Mum said it was a dog, but I don't see how a dog could do that.'

'And your sister thinks it's a wolf,' he said slowly, as if turning the image over in his mind.

'Oh, I'm sure she doesn't really think that. There are no wolves in this country.'

'There's none in Scotland anymore either,' said Gus. 'There used to be. Everywhere, they were, but people killed them off, hundreds of years ago now. So much of the old world is disappearing. The planet is dying. It's becoming dis-enchanted. Humans are killing it. Soon there'll be nothing left but the faerie realm. Unless the humans kill that too.'

'You seem to know a lot about the faerie realm. What do you think if it's not a wolf, or a dog? People?' That was the most likely. Nasty, horrible people, just as Gus had said earlier. She didn't want to think about it.

'Have you heard of a kelpie?'

It rang a bell. In a book on the shelf in the living room: a collection of stories about mythological creatures, she was sure of it. A picture came to her of a beautiful white horse, of children on its back. But then she thought of the lake monsters Grizzly had told them about to scare them away from going to the lake alone.

'Is it a horse? Or a monster?'

'It's not a monster,' insisted Gus. 'It's its own thing.

You would say it was a horse, yes. But it's more than a horse. It lives under the lake.'

'*Under* it? Not in it?'

'It's hard to explain — not under it exactly. It's beyond human ken. You can't use words to describe it.'

'You can use words to describe anything,' said Ella. 'Can't you?'

Gus laughed. 'That would be very convenient. But no, I don't reckon you can. This is the faerie realm, remember. It's not about language. Not any language you would understand, anyway. Not words.'

A door inside the house in her head creaked open then, and an image formed there of colour and light, green and gold. But it wasn't only an image. She felt it, too: a physical sensation in her body, and a musical refrain, just out of earshot; a smell. She tried to grasp it all, but it was gone. The door closed again. A taste lingered on her tongue, of mud and salt. She spat it out.

'Think of it like there's a thin membrane between this world and that. You can't see that other world but it's there. You can sense it sometimes, maybe. You seem like a clever girl.'

Ella thought about lying on the car with her father, the feeling she'd had of a veil hovering between her and the stars: order and calamity. She had thought she was on the side of order, but maybe she was wrong.

'What are you saying? That a kelpie killed the sheep?'

'A kelpie has to eat, just like anything else. At least it didn't kill a human, isn't that better?'

She cast her mind back; she was sure now that Grizzly had mentioned the kelpie as one of the multitude of creatures that could harm them if they wandered down to the lake on their own. Drown them, maim them — it was all the same nonsense.

'How come you know so much about it?' she said.

Gus shrugged. 'I keep my eyes and ears open.'

They reached the gate to the next paddock, the one Ella and Magpie liked to gallop in. She opened it, and let Storm and Gus through. Magpie flattened her ears when they got too close and shied away when Gus put out a hand to touch her.

'Funny wee ears she's got,' he said.

'Don't,' said Ella. 'She's got stranger danger, remember?' She said it lightly, but she was worried. She patted Magpie's neck and murmured to her. Magpie's little ears flicked back and forth, but she was jittery on her feet.

'I'll make friends with her,' said Gus. 'You'll see. She won't be able to resist me.'

'We don't have kelpies here,' continued Ella, as she leaned down to close the gate. 'This is another country, remember? It's already got its own lake creatures, if you believe in that sort of thing.'

'You'd be surprised,' said Gus. Then he cast her a mischievous look that said *ready?* and he took off as though he'd read her mind.

7

Jabble: agitation of water;
splashing in small ripples

Magpie hesitated as Storm surged ahead.

'Come on, Maggie!' Ella shortened her reins and squeezed her legs. Magpie snorted and gave a tiny buck. Ella nudged her with her heels and the pony gave up resisting and then she was thundering up the slope and there was nothing but the wind in their ears and the whipping of the tussock against Magpie's legs as they sliced through the landscape. Despite Magpie's size, and Storm's breeding, they soon caught up with Gus, who was crouched low, hands up near his shoulders, elbows at ninety degrees to his body, reins loose and uncontrolled.

The church came into view on the other side of the fence, and they slowed down to a walk, puffing, grinning, cheeks flushed.

'What kind of riding do you call that!' said Ella, laughing. 'You could take someone's eye out with those elbows.'

'You're just glumfie because we beat you,' said Gus. He moved closer, and Magpie danced away.

'Easy, girl,' Ella said, and took a deep breath in through her nose, then out through her mouth, pursing her lips, to see if it calmed her. Magpie was sweating hard, more than she usually would after a short gallop. Was it Ella herself making Magpie nervous? Horses could sense elevated heartbeats, interpreted them as danger. Was being around Gus making her own heart beat faster than usual?

'What are you doing?' Gus asked.

'I'm trying to calm her down. Did you know that a horse can hear a human heart beat four feet away?'

'Aye,' he said. 'Not only that. They can hear your blood tinkling in your veins. That's how a kelpie hunts, you know. It will hear you before you see it, and then it's too late for you.' He laughed a manic sort of a laugh.

'Enough with the kelpies,' she said.

'You should trust your horse,' he said. 'If she's nervous

about something, she probably has something to be scared about. Horses aren't like you. They can see danger in the darkest corners, dangers you're not even aware of.'

'Oversensitive you mean! Sir Ed, my mum's horse — he's scared of rabbits! Zippy's scared of puddles. He won't walk through them, has to go around them. He's a nightmare to ride after rain.'

'Well, maybe they know something you don't.'

'Maybe. Killer rabbits? Shark-infested puddles?'

They rode through another gate to where the church stood in the middle of a paddock. It was made of sandstone and blended into the tussocky landscape. There was a glaring great hole in the roof and the door stood open. A rowan tree, with white spring flowers and the last of the red berries gone, grew at an angle from a rock by the gate, which lay on the ground, torn from its rusted hinges. From here they could see the snowy mountains in the distance, and the lake wearing a bright blue cloak. If tourists got wind of the church, thought Ella, and the postcard scenery, it would be overrun.

'My nan used to like coming here,' she said. 'My grandad's buried here. It's so pretty. Look, it's a rowan. We've got one at home too. They must have missed that one when they were getting rid of them.'

'Nasty things,' said Gus. 'Who's getting rid of them?'

'They're a noxious weed around here. They used to grow all around the lake, but they got ripped up years ago. Grizzly thinks they grew from the one she planted when she arrived. To remind her of home, she said. But the birds got into the berries and carried them all over. She's supposed to be getting it chopped down but she hasn't got around to it yet.' Ella didn't say what she was thinking — that she'd had plenty of opportunity and was being stubborn. 'They're meant to protect against evil spirits or something.'

The day had warmed up. She removed her jacket and tied it around her waist. Then she leaned forward and kicked both feet out of the stirrups and jumped down. She moved to Magpie's head and patted her cheek, then led her over to the few scattered gravestones, all of them tarnished and lichen-covered.

Grandad's was the only grave from this century. Grizzly used to ride up here all the time when she was well enough, just to sit with it a while. She galloped up on Duke, her favourite, through the paddocks to the track, where he was as sure-footed as a goat. Ella had been with her a few times when she was younger, and she remembered the rowan in late summer with its berries blazing against a blue sky. But that was a long time ago now, and she couldn't remember the last time Grizzly had come, or when she'd last ridden a horse.

'How did he die?' asked Gus.

'He drowned, in the lake. In a Nor'wester. Grizzly warned him about going out, but he loved to fish. It happened before I was born. He went missing at first, but then he washed up on the shore a few days later.'

'Do you know what happened? How he drowned?'

Ella shrugged, but an image appeared, unbidden, in her mind. At first it was of a figure in a boat, far away, on the lake. The water was dark and choppy. Then the vision shifted, and she was inside the little dinghy, rowing, the Nor'wester singing in her ears. Rowing away from the rough waters and into the smooth emerald surface of the keld. The wind died away and the boat ceased its rocking to drift calmly. There was no sound but the gentle slap of water against the sides of the boat. A fishing rod appeared in her hand — but it wasn't her hand. It was weathered and brown, with stubby fingers and broken nails. The rod flicked a line over the side of the boat, and the sinker and bait dropped with a *ploop*.

Why was she seeing this? Ella shook her head, shook it away. She was back, standing with Magpie. Gus had dismounted, and Storm was cropping what grass he could find among the tussock.

'The usual way,' she said eventually. 'What do you mean?'

'I mean *do you know who drowned him?*'

Ella looked at Gus in horror. His face was as calm as you like, as if it was the most normal question in the world. She closed her eyes, and she was back on the boat, in the serene, still patch on the lake, while the rest of it was jabbly and shirred. And in the green depths, below the boat, a great shadow passed under her. There was a surge from beneath and the fishing rod fell from her hands . . .

Her eyes flew open and Gus was watching her, expectantly. Her legs wobbled.

'There was something in the lake,' she said, and her voice trembled.

Magpie threw up her head, agitated, ready to flee. Her heart . . . Maggie must be able to hear her heart . . . but *why*? She didn't know how, but she had a sudden certainty that her grandfather's drowning was not an accident. That some malevolent force, some *thing*, had come up under his boat and tipped him out, held him under, and drowned him.

'I . . .' She couldn't form words.

'The kelpie,' said Gus.

'But how . . . ?' She gaped at him.

He held tight to Storm's reins. He nodded soberly, but there was a look of something in his eyes. Amusement?

'Aye,' was all he said.

Jumbling in her mind was a thought. 'Did you put that there? Did you put that in my head?'

'I don't know what you mean,' he said. 'How could I do that? You've seen it for yourself. You've got a gift. Trust yourself.'

No, no, no. This couldn't be right. The image was tumbling around, getting tangled and mixed up with all her thoughts and her memories. She stamped her feet. 'Gah!' Why could she never order her thoughts? It was like a house in there, with different rooms. She could sometimes sense what was in each one, though they bled into each other through cracks under doors. There was always a room full of bees that she had to contend with, and keep tightly shut in, but they escaped all the time. In another an orchestra was always tuning up. Morag had taken her to a concert once, and when she'd heard the violins and the oboe and the clarinet all attempting to play the same note but slightly off-kilter, running up and down scales, she'd had a shock of recognition. It perfectly represented the noise and the chaos in her brain.

The image of the lake and the monster was fading, as so many of her memories did. She tried to hold it, but the door slammed shut and the handle disappeared, and the image was gone.

'What was it?' she said, emerging from a fog. 'What did you say? What were we talking about?'

Gus patted Storm on the shoulder and wouldn't look at her.

'Oh, you were just saying that your grandad drowned. And that nobody knows why.'

'Yes,' she said.

'And your nan, she comes up here and talks to him, does she?'

'She used to, before she got sick.'

'Heartbroken, was she? Or did she not really care for him?'

'Of course she cared for him! What a weird thing to say!' But Ella didn't know whether Grizzly had cared for him or not; she just assumed.

Gus didn't say anything but left Storm huffling around the ground looking for food. He wandered over to the headstone. He started singing a song, low, under his breath, and Magpie's ears flickered back and forth. The melody felt familiar to Ella, and she couldn't quite place it, until she could.

'My nan sings that song — where did you hear it?' It was the lament she'd heard Grizzly singing down by the lake, the song that ached and yearned for home, a home by another lake, a loch, somewhere on the other side of the world.

'Oh. It's just a wee ditty I heard somewhere.'

'Back in Scotland?'

'Maybe. What about your dad?' he asked. 'Where's he buried?'

Ella baulked, but hid it by leaning into Magpie's neck. She hadn't told Gus about her father's disappearance. One of the locals must have told him. In which case, he would know that he wasn't buried anywhere. And would know what other people around here thought of them. Her cheeks burned, but she didn't say anything, and he didn't press her.

Gus picked the melody up again, his voice low and sweet. It swirled in eddies around Ella, and she caught a glimpse of green light falling through water, felt a cool dampness against her skin. She had the distinct feeling that she was underwater, and that she wasn't alone, that someone was near. *Josh.*

She cried out.

Gus stopped singing. 'What is it?'

Her head bubbled, then settled. What was wrong with her today?

'Nothing,' she said, embarrassed. 'Let's go and look

in the church, see if Josh is in there.'

'You go,' said Gus. 'I'll wait here with the horses.'

But when she handed him Magpie's reins, her pony threw her head up and backed away. 'Stand still, you crazy devil,' he said, a hint of menace in his voice.

'It's okay,' said Ella. 'I'll tether her to the rowan. She won't go far if she can see me.'

Gus handed her back the reins, reluctantly, Ella thought, and she put a calming hand on her pony's neck before leading her to the front of the church and hanging her reins on a branch.

'I won't be long,' she murmured into the pony's ear, but when she stepped over the fallen gate, Magpie let out a whinny that said *come back soon*.

The door to the church stood ajar, and clusters of sheep pellets — poo — lay scattered on the doorstep like Hansel and Gretel's breadcrumbs.

Inside, the silence was overwhelming. The corners were filled with darkness, and she wondered momentarily if Magpie would find the hidden dangers lurking there, dangers outside of her own perception. She glanced away quickly, concentrating instead on a shaft of light that fell from the hole in the roof, illuminating the altar at the front of the church where the priest would have said his sermons all those years ago.

'Josh?' She called out in the gloom, but her voice was muffled. The air was thick with dust, and motes danced in the columns of light. She moved forward, looking at each pew in turn, searching for the shape of a boy lying down, sleeping. Or hiding. She made her way to the altar and looked up. The rafters were scribbled with nests, and a lone magpie leaned down, eyeing her with first one eye, then, with the turn of its head, the other. She'd heard of magpies swooping people's heads when they were nesting, and she didn't like the thought of that, but this one stayed where it was, watching. She thought of the magpies around her like witnesses: always there, always watching, always wanting a piece of the action.

The stillness was broken by an alarmed call from Magpie outside, a high-pitched whinny that reverberated through the church. Ella turned and ran back to the door. Magpie had torn herself free from the rowan and was now dancing, tossing her head, while Gus stood defiantly nearby, clutching his arm.

'Easy, girl,' said Ella, and at the sound of her voice Magpie calmed down, planting her hooves and turning to welcome her. Ella grabbed the reins that trailed dangerously.

'She bit me!' said Gus, disbelief written all over his face. 'That little devil bit me.'

'What were you doing? I told you she doesn't like people.' But Ella felt guilty and a bit desperate.

'I told you I was going to make friends with her. Horses like me.'

'And I told you, not this one. Why didn't you listen?'

He didn't answer, but his face grew dark, his teeth clenched, his thick black eyebrows almost obscuring his eyes. He took a sudden step towards Magpie, and she shied, dragging Ella with her. She cried out.

'I'm really sorry she bit you,' she said, her voice pleading. She had the sudden feeling that she needed to placate him, and she didn't like it, not when they had only just met and were getting on so well.

Gus rolled his sleeve back and examined his arm, looking for all the world like he'd never been hurt in his life. He stared at the red mark and rubbed at it, as though it was paint he could wipe away.

'You're fine,' said Ella. 'It'll just be a bit of a bruise.' She paused. 'Please don't tell my mum.'

Gus snapped his head up and looked at her. 'Oh, aye?'

'I don't want to give her a reason for keeping Magpie away from the treks. I'll never get to ride her if that happens. She might even send her away.'

'Sent away?' He thought about this. 'I won't tell her, Ella Ella.' His face had softened.

'Thank you.' At the sound of her name, the fear inside her had subsided, washed away. It was going to be fine.

'Did you find your lad?' he asked.

'Nothing but magpies.' She felt like there was something else she was going to say — it was on the tip of her tongue. A memory, a feeling, something important. She chased the thought, but it was gone.

THE HOUSE WAS QUIET when Ella got back, slamming the door behind her and leaving a trail of boots, jacket, gloves before she collapsed on the living-room couch. Fiona was out in the stone circle behind the house, where she liked to play games and look for treasure. Grizzly said the circle was natural, formed from limestone rocks rolling down off the hill, and that she had built the house next to it for luck. But it didn't look natural to Ella — someone must have put the stones there, a long time ago, she decided, and the earth and lichen had grown up around them, embedding them.

Grizzly was probably having an afternoon sleep, otherwise she would have been on the couch, reading a book or doing a crossword puzzle. The crossword book was on the table, next to Grizzly's notebook — her grimoire, her book of spells. Ella picked it up and opened it, smiling at Grizzly's scrawl. She recognised some of the words, but there were more she didn't know — *shadowtackle*, *holloway*, *susurrate*, *glisk*.

She put the notebook back, and cast her eyes over to the bookcase across the other side of the room. Books were stacked higgledy-piggledy — two deep in some places, vertical and horizontal — alongside pictures and knick-knacks, with Grizzly's antique iron sheep shears balanced precariously on top. She'd brought them all the way over from Scotland ('Still as sharp as the day they were made,' she told them proudly. 'Da could shear a hundred sheep before he'd need to sharpen those blades').

She found what she was looking for, its deep-green spine and gold lettering: *Scottish Mythical Creatures*. A memory stirred, of Grizzly sitting reading to her in bed. Wasn't this where she had seen the picture of the kelpie?

She crossed the room and picked the book up with both hands — it was heavy — and dropped it onto the couch with a puff of dust. It didn't take long to find the entry on the kelpie. Spread across the double page was the image she recognised, that she had loved looking at when she was smaller. The kelpie was a magnificent white horse, with a thick arched neck, high-stepping like a Lipizzaner, the Spanish show horse. Four children rode on its back, the one in front holding on to its mane as it sprang towards a body of water. To Ella, it had seemed such an idyllic image — the sun was shining, and she could imagine the thrill and enjoyment of riding a horse with three of her friends on its broad, rocking-horse back.

But now she saw something different. The children on the horse's back didn't look delighted. They looked alarmed. The one at the back, a little girl in an old-fashioned dress and a bonnet, looked downright terrified. Her face was stretched in horror, eyes shut and mouth wide open.

There was something else.

In the corner of the picture was another little boy cowering on the ground by a rock; he had dark hair and wore a grey jacket and shorts. In one hand he held a knife. His other hand hung by his side. Great drops of blood fell from the place where two of his fingers should be.

Ella dropped the book in horror. How did she not remember this? Why had she thought of it as a happy, playful image? Could it be that Grizzly had covered that part of the picture, showing her only the less disturbing part, which was painted in gentle, watery colours?

She read the brief story.

The kelpie lives in rivers and lakes in Scotland. It is a water sprite that takes the form of a beautiful horse on land and lures children onto its back, where they become stuck fast. The children are taken into the lake and drowned. Some say they are eaten, with only their livers washing up on the shore. In one version of the story, a little boy escapes by cutting off his own fingers, which have become tangled in the kelpie's mane. In another, the kelpie takes the form of a handsome man to lure women to their deaths. The story is thought to have been invented to keep children safe from drowning when their parents were busy toiling in the fields and unable to keep watch on them.

Ella got up and put the book back where she had found it. *It's just a story*, she told herself. *Just a story: nothing to worry about at all.*

8

Something woke her. A breath in the room, a sigh, a groan from outside? The sound of water, like a tap had been left running, or a waterfall. She lay in bed and listened for a moment. The air in her room was still and quiet. The sound came from outside.

Ella chucked back the covers and put her feet on the cold floorboards. Flexed her toes. She crossed to the window and pulled back the curtain.

In a silvery light, the black horse cantered lazily around the paddock. As Ella watched, its circles drew ever tighter. The other horses, all ten of them, formed a knot in the middle of the field, like a herd of sheep. Magpie let out an anxious whinny, but the rest were silent, all of them alert.

Around and around the stallion flew, its head and tail high. The only sound was its hooves on the grass, and somewhere the sound of running water. Ella stilled her breathing to listen harder. Her hand grew cold on the window latch.

She startled as something small and hard, like a pebble or a piece of gravel from the driveway, hit the window. She looked down. Standing below her window, looking up at her, was a dark human figure. Its arms were wrapped around itself as though it was freezing cold. Gus? No. *Josh*. His face turned up to her was blank; his hair dripped and water ran down his face as though he was standing under a shower. It poured from his body onto the gravel beneath his bare feet. He dropped his arms to his sides and stood and stared.

Ella followed her feet: she turned and ran for her door, wrenched it open and thundered down the stairs, calling out to her family, 'It's Josh! Josh is here!' She should have been happy to see him, relieved even, but all she felt was a creeping dread. She pulled open the front door.

The night outside was absolutely still. The hoofbeats had stopped. It was too dark to see. Where once there had been moonlight there was now only black. No stars, only an absence, like a great lid had been put on the valley. She ran outside in her bare feet, stones bruising her soles.

'Josh?' Her voice was small in the thick blackness.

He was nowhere to be seen.

She turned circles looking for him, and as she did so, she became aware of her feet, splashing through water. She was standing in a puddle that was growing ever larger. Ella turned and looked back at the house, expecting to see lights on, shouts, her mother pulling on her dressing gown to see what the commotion was about. But the house stood as quiet and dark as the surrounding night. She could just make out the one wilding pine, as tall as the house, and the dark shapes of roosting magpies. There was no sign of Josh. He was gone.

Puzzled, she sloshed back into the house. Her feet trailed water across the threadbare carpet. She tried to run, but her legs felt heavy. The bottom of her nightdress was weighted with water, and it was bringing her down, down towards the floor. She climbed the stairs on her hands and knees. At the top, she clambered to her feet and pushed open her mother's door.

'Mum?' Her mother didn't respond, just murmured in her sleep and turned over. Ella grabbed her shoulder and shook it gently. 'Morag!' Morag waved her hand as if swatting away a fly and smacked her lips like a baby, but didn't wake up. Ella backed away.

She tried Fiona's room next, and found her standing beside her bed.

'Did you see him?' said Ella. 'Josh?'

Her sister nodded. She raised her hand and pointed to the corner, behind the door. Ella turned.

Josh took a step forward, out of the shadows. His hair was sodden and laced with weeds. His face was pale and stricken, pleading for help. He opened his mouth as if to speak, but instead water poured out in a deluge, down his clothes and onto the floor.

Ella tried to scream, but it caught like a ghost in her throat.

She was sitting up in bed, back in her own room, and Josh was gone. She looked around wildly — how did she get back here? — and there was her bedspread, and her raincoat hanging off the coat-stand behind her door; pony posters on the wall; a jumble of books, toys and clothes making dark piles on the floor. The curtains were open and a thin grey light was spilling in. Somewhere she heard banging. It had been a dream then; she should have known. Her limbs moved when she asked them to; everything was in sharp focus. Her digital clock said it was 6.46 a.m.

The banging started up again — in the waking world. Someone was thumping on the front door, hard.

Morag came out of her room, shrugging on her dressing gown. 'Stay there,' she said. She looked worried, bleary-eyed, though she was usually up at this hour.

Ella hung back at the top of the stairs. Fiona appeared, clutching her rabbit and yawning. 'What's going on?' she said. Ella put her finger to her lips and indicated that Fiona should sit with her on the top step.

Morag opened the door. 'Hi, what's up?' they heard her say, straight to the point but wary — it's not every day someone bangs so hard on your door at dawn. She'd switched on the light downstairs, and the yellow wash climbed the wall beside them. Ella leaned forward to try to get a glimpse of who it might be, but Morag's body blocked the view.

'Have you seen him?' said a woman's voice. 'Have you seen Josh?'

'Come inside,' Morag said, and stood aside. Susan, Josh's mother, strode in. She looked wildly around the room, as if Josh might be hiding there somewhere, then her gaze travelled up the stairs to the girls. Ella flinched, but Susan looked away; they were not the child she was looking for. She wore a parka and gumboots, but didn't take them off now she was inside. Her mud-coloured hair was a scribble at the back of her head, held loosely with an elastic band. She clutched each elbow with the opposite hand, as though she was trying not to be sick. Her eyes found Morag again.

She repeated the question.

Morag turned her hands palms upward and shook her head. 'What's happened? Is there any news?'

Susan walked uninvited into the living area, and Ella heard the squeak of an armchair as she dropped into it.

Ella moved down two steps so she could watch what was going on. She could see the back of Susan's head over the top of the big leather armchair, the one that used to belong to her grandfather. Morag had moved to the nearby sofa, and was leaning as far forward as she could, her fingers entwined, her face open and waiting.

Susan's voice crackled. 'No, I'm such an idiot. This is ridiculous, but I had a dream. It was so real, and when I woke up I just had this strong feeling that he was here, or that you might know where he was. It was so real, Morag. He was standing in front of your house. He was soaking wet.'

Ella gasped. Fiona leaned into her and whispered in her ear, 'I had the same dream, Ellie. What does it mean?'

Ella turned to stare at her, but words wouldn't come. She was paralysed. Something like fear started in her scalp and poured through her body like cold water.

'It was only a dream,' said Morag, but something was wrong. She had jumped to her feet and wouldn't look at Susan. 'I'll put the kettle on.' Without waiting for a response, or even asking if Susan wanted a cup of tea, she went to the kitchen. Susan's head slumped forward, and over the rattle of mugs and the kettle coughing to life, the sound of soft sobs rose around her.

Why was Morag behaving so strangely? She should have been beside her neighbour, offering her a hug or a calming hand on her shoulder; instead she was banging around in the kitchen as if she was avoiding something. Ella couldn't help herself. She pushed off from the step and went slowly down the stairs. The banister was cold and smooth under her hand. Fiona followed her.

She went to the back of Susan's chair and put her hand on her shoulder. The woman startled and glanced around at Ella as though she'd felt something ghostly. But her features settled again and she brought a hand up to make a show of rubbing at her forehead, when really she was hiding her face. She took deep breaths, trying to calm herself down. Head bent, she fumbled in her pocket and brought out a thin, crumpled tissue to spread out and blow her nose on.

Ella had seen this before. This grief. Josh's mother seemed so raw, so naked. It was hard to know where to look, and she understood why her mother might have walked away. All the turmoil of the last few days was right there on the surface, and here Susan was in a strange house. Ella had seen the face before, on her own mother, at the police station the day her father had disappeared.

Suddenly, Fiona was there, pushing Ella aside and putting her arms unbidden around Susan's neck. She hated to see people upset. She felt it deep inside herself, and her first instinct was always to try to make others feel better. Ella was never sure whether it was to soothe the person or to soothe Fiona herself, because if they felt better, Fiona felt better.

'Oh,' said Susan. She was slow to respond, but when Fiona didn't let go, she raised her hands and patted her back. Then she relaxed and accepted the hug. Fiona pulled away. 'Thank you,' said Susan, though her voice was wary. She stood up, apparently unsettled by finding herself alone with the two children, one stubborn with set features, the other the strange little girl with the white eyelashes. She walked over to the kitchen bench, where Morag was pouring water into two mugs, strings and tags of tea bags hanging over their rim.

'I don't want tea, Morag,' she said, and folded her arms, planted her feet. 'I want you to talk to me.'

Morag put the kettle down. 'Of course,' she said. 'Sorry.'

'I need to ask you what you know about Josh and where he is.'

'But Susan, I don't know anything. Less than you probably!'

Susan's cheeks were flushed. She took a gulp of air.

'Is this about Ross, and wanting you off the land?'

Ella remembered then, the earlier confrontation, when Josh's father had bundled himself into the Land Rover, slamming the door. She heard Josh's voice in her ear: *My dad says you're a house of witches and you can't pay your rent.* Except it wasn't about not being able to pay rent. Josh's dad wanted to install a huge dairy farm right next door, and had hoped to use the land the trekking stables sat on for irrigation pipes to the monstrous machines that would turn the golden landscape into unnatural circles of green.

Grizzly had refused to move, but she'd done more: when the bulldozers turned up to flatten the side of the Ben to make way for a dairy platform, she'd brought in protesters from all around the country to chain themselves to the machinery. The publicity had forced the local authorities to shut the venture down. Potential jobs evaporated with it.

Grizzly had saved the landscape and the lake from pollution, but the fallout for the family had been severe. All these years later, they still had few friends in the Basin.

'Of course not,' said Morag. 'Whatever problems we've had with Ross have got nothing to do with Josh.

And this — Josh going missing, whatever — has nothing to do with us.'

'I know you don't like him.'

'What are you talking about? He's a kid! I hardly know him. I have no opinion of him either way.'

'I know that he's been bullying Fiona, and Ella too.'

'Well . . .' Morag glanced at the girls helplessly. Ella nodded. 'Well, that may be so, but I don't know what that has to do with him disappearing.'

'No?' said Susan. She moved forward and placed both hands on the bench. 'People do seem to disappear around here, though, don't you think?'

'What do you mean?' Morag stepped back in shock.

'The menfolk. Around you and your mother. First your dad, then your husband. Gone. Poof! Without a trace.'

'And you think we had something to do with that?'

'Hitting you, was he?' Susan's voice had raised a level in pitch. 'Bullying you?'

'Stop it,' said Morag. Her face had gone a dark shade of red.

'And your girls now.' She reached into her pocket. 'What's this, hm? I found it at the end of our driveway. And you've got one like it at the end of yours.' She pulled something out and threw it on the bench. It clattered and skittered to rest next to where Morag was leaning. She picked it up. It was one of Fiona's creations. Ella could guess what it was made of. Probably a bird skull, a twist of sheep's wool, a sprig of thyme, a shell from her collection. Tied together with string.

'It's . . . it looks like one of Fiona's artworks.'

'*Artworks!* Is that what you call them? They look more like witchcraft to me.'

Morag threw a glance at Fiona, who was trembling next to Ella. Then Fiona turned and fled up the stairs.

'Go with her, Ellie,' Morag said.

Ella was torn. She wanted to comfort Fiona, but more than that she wanted to hear what Susan had to say.

Morag turned her attention back to her neighbour. 'Listen to yourself, Susan. *Witchcraft*. You're being ridiculous.'

'Don't play dumb.' Susan's shoulders were set in an ugly, determined stance. 'Everybody knows what goes on out here. What's always gone on, you and your mother. Nobody's ever seen you at church on Sunday. Now raising your two girls to follow in your footsteps. If you don't like the men in your life, you just get rid of them!' She was shouting now. 'Will was well-liked in this community until you set your sights on him. Well, I'm not afraid of you! Give me back my son! I know you

91

know where he is!' She picked up one of the mugs, still steaming, and threw it on the ground, where it bounced but didn't break. Hot tea splashed up the side of her gumboots.

'Enough!' A voice came from the hallway that led to the downstairs bathroom and to Grizzly's room. She was standing there, holding on to the door handle as if it was all that was supporting her. Susan stopped and stared. Grizzly was wearing her worn robe, open to reveal flannelette pyjamas. Her white hair flew wildly around her head. Her eyes were on fire — they were enough to stop a bull dead in its tracks.

She raised a hand and pointed at Susan. 'You. I know you're grieving, and for that I'm sorry. But you do not come into my house and start accusing my daughter and me and those sweet innocent children of things like witchcraft. Using the death of our loved ones against us like that. You should be ashamed of yourself. I hope it's just the grief talking. Now get out of my house, and go and talk to the police if you think you have any proof of anything. I hope you find your lad, I really do. I would never wish on you what we have gone through in this house. But just leave now.'

It seemed to wake Susan up. She looked down at her body as if surprised to find herself standing in the house, on a dirty patch of carpet where mud had fallen from her boots and mixed with the spilt tea. She looked up again, stricken. 'I'm sorry.' Shame burned red across her features. 'I'm sorry,' she repeated, and she turned, and all but ran from the room. She left the front door open behind her and the next moment they heard the four-wheel drive start up, tyres spinning on the gravel and the engine revving away down the driveway.

Morag saw Ella still standing in the living room. 'Go,' she said, and it was the only word Ella needed. She ran up the stairs two at a time to Fiona's room as Morag dropped a tea towel and bent to clean up the sodden, dirty floor.

9

Waukenin: a reprimand; a reproof

Ella found Fiona back in her bed with the covers pulled up over her head, crying noisily. Ella remembered the word for it — like a gust of wind and rain, a fit of crying. A blirt.

So as not to startle her, Ella tapped softly on her open door, said her name once, then walked over to her bed and crouched down beside her. She laid a hand on where she thought her shoulder was under the blanket.

'I'm going to pull the blanket back now, okay?'

Fiona went rigid and answered with a shrill squeal, which was how she rejected an idea when she was too exhausted or too overwrought to speak.

Ella waited, leaving her hand where it was so that her sister knew she hadn't abandoned her.

After a few minutes Fiona went quiet and still, and Ella wondered if she had fallen asleep, but then the covers moved and Fiona's hands appeared, scrabbling at the blankets, followed by her face flushed pink and sweaty. She stuck out her bottom lip and blew — a cool wind on Ella's face, no more than a whiffle.

'Okay?' said Ella. 'Ready to talk?'

Fiona's face crumpled a little and she stared off into the corner of the room.

'If you painted a picture of how you felt right now, what would it look like?'

Fiona thought for a moment. 'I'd paint a tree. With water colours.'

'Yeah? What kind of tree?'

'A tree without leaves.'

'Like in the winter?'

'Yes. And a bench for sitting on. Except nobody would be sitting on it.'

'So an empty bench. Got it.'

'And the tree and the bench would be under a big watery sky.'

'That's how you're feeling right now?'

Fiona nodded.

'I get it.' They'd been making pictures out of their feelings for a long time. Sometimes describing the picture was easier than describing the feeling inside.

'I was just trying to keep them safe,' Fiona said in a small voice.

'Keep them safe,' Ella repeated. 'What do you mean?'

'With the charm. I made it for them, to keep them safe. To bring Josh home. Even though I didn't like him. I made one for us too. I put them at the end of our driveways.'

'When did you do that?' It was a long walk to the Underhills' letterbox.

'Yesterday. Hana drove me down there.'

Ella pictured them in the little hatchback, Hana's neat head above the steering wheel, Fiona's small blonde one under the hood of her yellow raincoat, barely seeing over the dashboard.

'She was wrong, Ellie. I didn't like him, but I wouldn't hurt him.' She paused as another thought came to her. 'I wouldn't even know how.'

'I know.' Ella patted her hand. 'She gets that now. She didn't know what she was talking about. You should have seen the right *waukenin* Grizzly gave her!'

Fiona smiled at Ella's use of one of Grizzly's words, but Ella grimaced inwardly at remembering the shame

96

that had come over Susan, the pain that had shown on her burning face as she ran out. Ella couldn't imagine what she must be feeling.

Fiona fiddled with the elastic band around Ella's wrist, concentrating on it very hard as she whispered, 'You had the dream too, didn't you?'

Ella nodded. 'What did you see in your dream?'

'He was standing in my room, in the corner by the door. You came in and turned and looked. He was wet — there was water coming out of him. Out of his mouth.'

'Oh.' Ella felt all the puff go out of her. 'Mine was the same. Then the banging started and I woke up.'

Fiona just nodded. 'What does it mean? Is it something to do with the horse? The black horse? I heard hoofbeats in my dream too, I'm sure of it.'

'I don't know.' Ella felt helpless. 'You've seen the black horse too?'

Fiona nodded. 'We should ask Grizzly.' She clamped her eyebrows down and nodded. 'She'll know. She knows things.'

'Don't say that out loud!' Ella surprised herself with a giggle. 'People will start calling her a witch.'

'Oh, Ellie,' said Fiona. 'They already do, didn't you know that?'

She did.

A STUNNED PALL LAY over breakfast. Grizzly sat at the table with them. There was too much to process.

'You know she was wrong, don't you?' said Morag. 'That thing she said. About your dad.'

Ella and Fiona just nodded.

'She was right about one thing though,' said Ella. 'People don't like us.'

'Ach!' said Grizzly. 'What would they know? Suspicious minds, the lot of them. They don't deserve us.'

'Why don't they like us?' asked Fiona. Her eyes were wide. She stared at her cornflakes as if they held all the answers she needed.

Morag looked at Grizzly, who nodded.

'Your nan did a very brave thing,' said Morag. 'Years ago now. But it didn't make her many friends, and as a consequence it didn't make us many friends either. This place is small. People stick together. They talk. They're like a bunch of gossiping ostriches.'

'With their heads in the sand?' asked Fiona.

'That's exactly right,' said Grizzly. 'They wanted jobs, yes. Fair enough. But at what cost? The big dairy farms they were planning on putting in around here — they would have ruined this place. The lake, the Ben. We have to protect what's wild or it'll all be spoilt.'

'But why did she say that thing about Dad?' asked

Ella. 'About whether he was hitting you? And why did Josh say everyone knows you're witches?'

'That is just pure spite, that is,' said Grizzly. 'They're scared of a house full of strong women, just as they were scared of strong women centuries ago. Do you know they used to drown women they accused of being witches? They dropped them in the loch to see if they'd float. If they did, and they didn't drown, that proved they were witches and they burned them at the stake. And if they did drown? They were innocent. But dead. Some things never change.'

'Don't worry,' Morag said quickly, eyeing Fiona, whose cheeks had grown pink. 'They don't do that now. And your dad was the gentlest man I ever met.' Her voice cracked, but her face stayed like stone.

'Aye, but the sentiment is there. Small minds.' Grizzly rolled her eyes.

'Mum . . .' said Ella. 'You had it too, didn't you? The dream.'

Morag said nothing. She spooned her last spoonful of porridge into her mouth, stalling.

Everyone watched her, waiting.

'Fine,' she said eventually. 'I had a dream about Josh. So what? Everybody dreams.'

'But I had the same dream,' said Ella. 'So did Fi.'

'Aye,' said Grizzly. 'I had it too.'

'With the horse?' asked Fiona.

'You saw a horse? I thought that was just me. I knew a horse like that once, a long time ago.'

'It's been hanging around here lately,' said Ella. 'I've seen it twice now. But how did it turn up in your dream if you haven't seen it? Have you seen the horse, Mum?'

'No, but you told me about it. It was only my brain reminding me, that's all. You know what dreams are — just our brains making sense of our thoughts. I'll ask around about it.'

'But what does it mean that we all had the same dream?' asked Fiona.

'Nothing,' snapped Morag. She stood abruptly, shoving her chair back. 'It's a coincidence.'

'Well, the boy's no' here, anyhow,' said Grizzly with a false brightness. 'That poor family and what they're going through. If anything, we know more than anyone how they're feeling, so we'll think nothing but kind thoughts.'

'I put a curse on him, Grizzly.' Ella pushed her empty bowl away.

'No, you didn't, silly. Saying the words don't make it a curse. That lad was trouble, but he couldn't help it with the nonsense his parents were no doubt feeding him.

He didn't deserve to disappear, and you didn't make it happen. Just remember that. And remember that we are just a normal family, trying to get on with life, like everyone else.'

She didn't sound like she believed it, and Ella thought there was something she wasn't saying. Grizzly's face had the look of one who was miles away from here, thinking about another time and place.

'All right,' said Morag. 'Those horses aren't going to get themselves groomed and tacked up. We've got a lake-side trek due in an hour. Come on, Ellie, get dressed and be ready to go in five minutes. Once they're in, you can help too, Fifi.'

ELLA WAS IN the tack room cleaning metal bits when she heard a car door slam and loud voices outside. She'd been thinking about the day before, about Gus, but the details were foggy, like she'd forgotten some of it. It had been fun, though, and she was already planning where the two of them might ride to next. Around the lake maybe. They could take some sandwiches; make a day of it. She realised that she'd been waiting years for a friend to go riding with, had never dared hope she'd find one.

They'd keep looking for Josh, of course — she felt

guilty for a moment that she was thinking about Gus instead. But what was it he'd said? Something about the lake? She was sure it related to Josh somehow, to his disappearance. Did he have a theory? She tried to sift around in her head, but the memory seemed only to have left a sort of impression, like an evaporating ring of water on a table.

Hana went to greet the visitors as usual: four young men and a silent, watching young woman with dead straight hair that hung around her face. She had her hood up and had pulled the sleeves over her hands. They had told Hana they were experienced riders and were looking to go for a 'good hard gallop'. Hana had humoured them, but she and Morag didn't make the horses gallop with riders they didn't know; it was too risky. The horses would get competitive and try to race each other, and the riders could lose control. But they'd get a good solid canter across the paddock heading away from home. Not on the way back to the stables, though. That could spell disaster.

The men — overgrown boys, really, with caps pulled low over their eyes — were boisterous, broad-shouldered, slapping each other on the back and swearing at each other good-naturedly but with an aggressive edge that Ella could hear from the barn. Morag strode over and gave them a sharp word before walking away, probably before she said something she'd regret. They nodded solemnly but elbowed each other and made faces of mock shame when she made her way back to the house.

Hana came into the tack room, rolling her eyes.

'Let's grab the helmets for these idiots and get going. I'm not sure they're as experienced as they say, or if they're all farm boys moved to the city. Boy racers.'

As they emerged from the barn, there was a commotion: a gale of laughter, a 'Go, Dominic!' followed by a clatter of hooves. Ella saw the bustle before she registered what was happening. One of the men was sitting on top of Magpie — but not for long. He was ridiculously too big for her. His city shoes were crammed into her stirrups, which had been set for Ella's height, and his jeaned legs were crooked so far he looked like a jockey. Ella was just in time to see his expression of mischief — what a hoot! — shift to alarm as Magpie reared up, snapping the twine her lead rope was tethered to. Dominic leaned forward and grabbed her mane while his friends gasped and whooped, agitating Magpie even more.

She reared again, higher, and this time he couldn't stay on. He fell off the back of her, hitting a water trough on his way down with a resounding thud. Magpie wheeled around and reared again, and for a moment it looked like she was going to bring her front legs down on him, but he curled into a terrified ball and she missed him. She backed off, trembling all over, eyes so wide they were rimmed with white. Dominic's friends had gone silent now, and the girl had her hands over her mouth, staring in horror at the crumpled figure on the ground.

Hana put a hand out, palm up, towards the group. 'Stand still!' she said, and to Ella hissed quietly, 'Go, get her, *now*.'

Ella nodded and held her breath. She walked slowly towards her horse, who had got herself in such a frenzy that her neck was flecked with foam. Magpie startled, her hooves making a clatter on the concrete of the yard, and Ella thought that was it — she was going to take off, make for the road, a car would come—

She pushed that out of her head and concentrated on Magpie in front of her.

'Easy, girl,' she said.

At the sound of her voice, Magpie's small ears flickered and she stopped moving. In the silence, Ella could hear Dominic groaning.

Ella edged closer, murmuring all the while, 'Good horse, there's the good horse, you're okay, girl, you're okay.'

Magpie gave a soft nicker, and when Ella grabbed the

lead rope the pony put her head down and nudged her in the stomach. Ella led her quickly away, and Magpie followed obediently, calm now, as though the storm she had just unleashed had never happened at all. Ella felt a cold finger of fear creep into her stomach then, not of Magpie, not even for the man lying on the ground, clutching his arm, pale as salt. She was scared of what was to come, and what the consequences would be.

10

The best place for Magpie was in the home paddock, so Ella quickly removed her saddle, bridle and halter, then turned her out. Magpie, perhaps still working out the kinks of tension, galloped away across the field, leaping and kicking, twisting in the air. On another day, Ella would see it as a joyful and rambunctious celebration of life, and it would make her laugh. Today she felt only dread, and saw, through Hana's eyes, a dangerous and possibly deranged horse that would have no place in a trekking business. Hana would have to tell Morag. She couldn't bear it.

But when Ella came back to the yard, Morag, who could always sense trouble with the horses no matter where she was, was already there. The sullen, hunched girl was now screaming at her. Hana was on the ground next to Dominic, administering first aid. The remaining horses were shuffling in place, slightly agitated but as unflappable as ever.

'That crazy horse should be put down!' The girl had her hood back now, and was standing up straight, one hand on her hip, the other waggling in Morag's face.

Morag's expression remained stony. 'He shouldn't have been on that horse, and he knows it.'

Dominic looked guilty as charged. 'Ruby . . .' he said, but his voice trailed away. He was still pale, like he might throw up at any moment.

'That boy told him to get on her, it's not his fault,' insisted Ruby.

'What boy?' said Morag.

'The one who works here.' She looked around. 'Where is he?'

'There are no boys working here,' said Morag. 'It must have been one of your own.'

'Are you calling me a liar?' said the girl.

'Look, that doesn't matter right now,' Hana said from where she crouched. 'We need to get Dominic into town. I'm pretty sure his arm is broken.' She was trying to put ice on it, but Dominic kept flinching and pulling away. 'It'll be quicker to drive him than wait for an ambulance.'

'You see!' cried Ruby. 'We'll shut you down. You don't deserve to run a trekking business.'

A flush crept up Morag's neck. She took a step back as though to stop herself from reacting physically to Ruby's threat.

'We have strict health and safety protocols,' she said. 'You accept that while you are in our care you follow all our instructions or we won't be responsible for the consequences. Your friend broke those protocols, and while I'm sorry for him, he should not have been on that horse. That horse is my daughter's horse, and he should not have even approached it, let alone without a helmet. Horses are not robots, you know.' Her voice was getting louder; she was starting to lose her cool. 'They're animals. They react to being badly treated as surely as you or me.' She crossed her arms and dared the girl to respond.

'Well,' Ruby huffed. 'I don't know what's happened to that kid, but he was definitely here before. We'll give you a bad review anyway. Warn everyone you have psycho horses, and a psycho owner as well.'

'You do that,' said Morag. 'Now, do you want us to take your friend here to the clinic in our van, or do you want to drive him yourself?'

* * *

THE TREK WAS CANCELLED, and Morag felt she had no choice but to give the clients a refund. Ruby had opted to drive Dominic herself, and the rest of the party slunk away, though they couldn't resist squealing their tyres at the end of the driveway, zooming off in a puff of smoking rubber which lingered as a sour stink long after they were gone.

Ella could tell Morag was angry with her by the way she didn't yell at her. She just went quiet, head down, moving around the horses, taking off their tack with a jerk, brushing them down using all her muscles. She didn't look at her daughter or even speak to Hana. Ella wished she would just scream at her and get it over with, though she wasn't exactly sure it was her fault. But she well knew they couldn't stand to lose the money from an afternoon's trek.

Hana stayed out of Morag's way after that, and jumped up in relief when her afternoon private lesson arrived — a woman Morag's age who had recently rediscovered the joys of riding. They led Zippy, the dappled grey, off into the training ring, chatting about the weather and how sore the woman was after their last lesson. Hana had to be vigilant around Zippy — he was a great horse to ride, if a little slow, but he tended to try to nip anyone who was on the ground, and he didn't like getting his feet wet.

Ella and Fiona's job was to clean up the *doofers* — horse poo — after the lesson. They shovelled it into a huge pile behind the barn and sold it by the sackful as garden fertiliser, leaving it at the end of the driveway with an honesty box for payment. There was always less money in there than there should have been — Ella wondered if maybe people around here weren't that honest, or liked to find small ways to insult them. Shovelling poo was hardly her favourite task, but today she was glad to get away from the black cloud of her mother for a bit.

THAT NIGHT, AT DINNER, Morag fixed Ella with a calm look.

'We're going to talk about what happened today,' she said.

Ella looked down at her mashed potato and moved some peas on top of it. She pushed the peas into the creamy mess and watched them disappear.

'Do you understand why I was upset?'

Ella nodded. 'Of course. But it wasn't my fault,' she added quickly, excavating one of the peas and popping it into her mouth.

'This isn't about blaming anyone, Ella. That boy was

110

an idiot. But as a business we have to be idiot proof. We can put all these health and safety protocols in place, but if our clients act like fools before they've even signed the agreement, it's another risk I have to factor. This trekking business is our livelihood. If we lost our licence, what would we do?'

'Hey now,' chipped in Grizzly, who had roused herself to sit with them at the table in her dressing gown. 'You sound like you are blaming the lassie. Just listen to the tone of your voice.'

'No,' said Morag. 'No. I'm not blaming her. I'm trying to make her understand why I'm going to say what I'm about to say.'

Ella's face felt hot suddenly. She felt her blood pulsing in her temples. She put her fork down.

It was Fiona who piped up and said what Ella was thinking but didn't dare say aloud.

'You're not going to kill Magpie, are you?'

'Fiona! No. *No.* Look, we've had accidents before. They happen. But I'm worried that word will get around that our horses are dangerous, and people will stop coming. It could have been much worse. He wasn't wearing a helmet — he could have banged his head. Luckily it was his arm that took the fall and not his skull, or there'd be a lot more trouble. But we have to face the fact, Ella, that

111

Magpie is dangerous. What if it had been Fiona?'

Fiona, who had separated her meat, vegetables and potatoes, was now eating her peas diligently without involving herself in the discussion further.

'Magpie loves Fiona!' cried Ella. It was true. She'd felt a twinge of jealousy more than once as Fiona sang to the pony and plaited her forelock. 'And she knows not to ride her. Only I ride her.'

'Well, Magpie won't be allowed on treks anymore. I can't take the risk of something like this happening again.'

'Ma!'

'No, don't argue with me. The alternative is getting rid of her altogether. Sending her somewhere she's not a menace to the public.'

'But you need me on the treks, don't you?' Surely Morag couldn't deny that.

'You can ride one of the other horses. Rocky, or Joey. You can ride Magpie in your own time. Where I can see you. I don't trust that horse.'

Suddenly Ella wasn't hungry anymore. She pushed her chair back and stood up.

'I didn't say you could leave the table.'

Ella ignored her, turned and ran for the stairs, taking them two at a time.

Grizzly's voice, soft, followed her. 'You're being a bit harsh on the poor lassie, aren't you?'

Ella slammed her door before she heard her mother's answer. She threw herself on her bed, buried her head in her pillow and sobbed.

After a few minutes she heard her door being pushed gently open. But it wasn't her mother come to apologise, it was Fiona. She had something in her hand. Without a word, she put it on Ella's bedside table, pushing aside books and cups to make a clear spot. She patted Ella on the shoulder and left the room.

11

Ella must have cried herself to sleep. In her dreams, a dark waterfall poured down off the Ben and into the blue lake, churning it to black, poisoning it. As she watched, she realised it wasn't water but a pack of animals, grey with fiery eyes and sharp teeth, thousands of them. Wolves. Fiona was riding on the back of the last one, crouched low, and Ella cried out just as the wolf leapt into the lake and was gone, taking her sister with it.

She woke early to an impossibly loud dawn chorus. She still wore her clothes from the night before; whether she had crawled under the covers herself, or someone had tucked her there, she couldn't be sure.

She heaved herself up and went to the window, opening the curtain a crack to peer out. An eerie wash of grey greeted her. In the paddock, dark shapes of the horses moved gently about. She opened the window. The shrill bell of the magpies' song enveloped her, notes that rose and fell like syllables of warning, bouncing around the paddocks and up to her window. Through the cacophony, she heard a heartfelt nicker that could only have come from Magpie, as if the pony sensed her there, in the silver morning.

Yesterday's events came back to her then, and a great sigh erupted out of her. She needed to be with her pony.

She had another thought: what if she could find Josh? Her mother couldn't be mad with Magpie if the pony led her to a missing boy, could she?

The first trek was not till eleven, so she had plenty of time. As quietly as she could, she pulled on warm pants and woollen socks, her favourite knitted jersey and her padded vest. It wouldn't be long before her mother was up, getting the porridge on. She ran her brush through her hair but hit thick knots. She grimaced at herself in the mirror. When was the last time she had brushed it? Days ago, probably. She put the brush back down again. She could do it later.

Ella crept down the stairs. She left a note on the

kitchen bench, got her boots and hat from by the back door, then headed out, patting her pockets — sure enough, she'd left her gloves behind. She'd need them this morning. Back up the stairs, into her room: a morning ritual repeated too often — there was always something she'd forgotten. When she was younger, Morag had written a list of things Ella needed to get or do every morning — including brushing her hair and teeth — and pinned it to the wall, but Ella had pulled it down a couple of years later. It was baby stuff.

As she grabbed her gloves from the bedside table, something caught her eye. She scooped it up, looking at it closely. Fiona's charm, the one Susan had thrown on the counter, hung like a necklace, spinning on its string: feather, bone, stone and rowan sprig. She remembered the day her father found the frog bones, picked clean by ants; how he counted them out into her hand. She was glad Fiona had taken to them. She hung the charm — or was it a talisman? — on her dressing-table mirror to keep it safe.

Outside, she crunched around the side of the house furthest from her mother's bedroom. It was growing lighter by the minute and her breath was visible in front of her. The cold wouldn't last once the sun was up. In the paddock, mist poured from the swampy earth, rising upwards like smoke. The horses stood knee deep in it.

Into the barn, grabbing a halter and a carrot from the huge sack by the door, and then she was in the paddock. The mist played tricks on her eyes, wisping and dissipating into fingers of light as she moved through it, making the grass undulate. It's no wonder people believed in ghosts, she thought, when nature put on a spectral show like this.

Magpie came to her, ears pricked, nuzzling her hand for the morsel and standing still, crunching, while Ella threw her arms around her neck and buried her face in her mane, sniffing her horsey smell.

Beyond the paddock she thought she saw a dark shape moving in the fog, and started, but it swirled and dissolved. Nothing but a *grumma* — a mist mirage. More spectres.

'Come on, Maggie,' she whispered, 'we have to be quick.'

Even though she had left a note, she had a feeling Morag wouldn't want her out here on her own, not with children going missing, so she wanted to make sure she was long gone before anyone stopped her. After all, if she couldn't ride on her own, when would she ever be able to ride her beloved pony? Her mother wouldn't go with her — she was far too busy. Hana couldn't because she was paid to work, not babysit. This was the only way. She would only be gone an hour and then she'd be back to face the consequences.

Ella took off Magpie's cover, gave her a quick brush down, and had her tacked up in record time. The roke was thinning and the sun was starting to rise above the far mountains, flushing the sky blood orange.

'*Red sky in the morning, shepherd's warning.*' She muttered the old rhyme to Magpie as she swung up on to her back and guided her to the grass verge beside the driveway to make as little sound as possible. Just in time — the light in Morag's bedroom was on and she would soon find the note.

Magpie's ears pricked forward and her step was high and eager. Ella sang softly under her breath and watched her pony's ears flicker back and forth. Magpie's head swung as she watched the landscape come alive. A small brown speckled pipit hopped along beside them, flapping its wings to keep up before giving up and falling back.

A magpie strutted out of their way, and Maggie pretended to shy at her namesake.

'Hello, Mr Magpie, how's your wife?' sing-songed Ella.

Light grew on the sparsely treed landscape, and the Ben, glowing pink now, watched them with a friendly eye. 'Can't keep up with your moods,' said Ella. Today was going to be a good day, she thought, pushing aside the idea of facing her mother on her return. High above them, a skylark trilled as it made its long ascent into the clouds. Soon it would drop back to earth, scooping the air with its wings just before it hit the ground.

As she came to the road at the end of the driveway, Magpie snorted and stopped.

A figure moved from beside the letterbox.

'Hey,' said Gus. 'Hope I didn't startle you.' The morning light fell on his face. He was dressed in the same oversized jacket and beanie pulled low over his eyebrows.

Magpie flattened her ears and walked back a few steps, her shoes ringing on the driveway. She huffed.

Ella tightened her grip on the reins as she recalled Dominic falling and hitting the trough. Is this how it would be now? Scared of encountering people in case Magpie injured them? Her pony felt tense below her, quivering. She'd never been this nervous before. It must have been the trauma of the day before — she'd lost what little trust she had in humans other than Ella.

'Everything all right?' asked Gus. 'Not going to bite me again, is she?'

'I hope not.' Ella debated whether to tell him about yesterday's incident, but decided he didn't need to know. 'What have you been up to?'

'Oh, this and that. What about you? What's happened since I last saw you? I thought I might see you out on your pony.'

'I couldn't yesterday.'

'Have you heard anything about that boy? Josh?'

'No. But something weird happened.' She told him about her dream, about Susan visiting. She didn't mention the horse.

'They're bad news, that family,' said Gus, scowling. 'Whatever's happened to him, don't you think they might have deserved it?'

'What do you mean? Why?'

'He was a real bully to you and your sister, wasn't he? And as for his father — trying to get you all off your land just to pollute the lake with that big dairy farm.'

Ella stared at him. Had she told him about the bullying? About the dairy farm?

'Have you been watching us or something?' she said eventually — half joking, but also not.

'You told me. Don't you remember?'

'No,' she said, truthfully. 'But I guess that's not unusual for me.' Something nagged at her, though — this didn't feel the same as forgetting what Morag had asked her to do, or leaving her gloves behind.

Magpie shifted beneath her, nodded her head,

straining against her hands. She wanted to get going.

'I saw you yesterday, though,' said Gus. 'I know what happened with her.' He nodded towards Magpie, keeping a safe distance. 'How she nearly killed that man.'

'You were there?'

'I was near.'

Ella remembered, then, what the girl Ruby had said. *That boy told him to get on her . . . The one who works here.*

'Did you tell him to get on Magpie?'

'Why would I do that? Not when she's so dangerous. Not when you said your mother would send her away. Why would I do that?'

His saying it again didn't make Ella more confident that he hadn't. Why *would* he do that? Revenge? She couldn't name what she felt in that moment, but she thought it may have been disappointment.

'Look,' said Ella. She twisted in the saddle to look back over the house. Smoke rose from the chimney and lay across the roof in the still air. 'I have to go. I'm going to keep looking for Josh. That dream made me think that he's still alive. Down by the lake maybe.'

'You still want to find him?'

'I don't know. Yes?' She didn't sound as sure as she felt, but she also didn't tell him that she still felt responsible for Josh's disappearance, despite what Grizzly had said.

'We've got a trek later and I have to be back for it.'

'Your ma's letting you take her on a trek?'

'No.' She gave a bitter half-laugh. 'That's why I'm riding her now.'

'Can I come with you? I could go and grab Storm quickly now.'

His eagerness was unsettling. 'No, I'm in a hurry today,' said Ella. 'Come by some other time.'

He didn't look happy with that idea, and sighed theatrically. 'Say . . .' He pointed at the letterbox. Hanging from the latch was one of Fiona's talismans, twisting gently. A delicate skull of some small mammal, probably a stoat, some more rowan. 'Did you make that?'

'No, my sister Fiona made it. It's a hobby.' She shrugged.

'Is she a witch?' It sounded like 'wutch' in his accent.

Not him too. Had he been talking to other kids? So soon? Couldn't she just have one friend untainted by local gossip?

'No,' said Ella, shrugging and — she couldn't help herself — scowling. 'The opposite, I think. Whatever that is. It's supposed to keep us safe from evil, or something. I think she put it here when Josh went missing. She tried to leave one at the Underhills' but Susan brought it back.' Threw it back, more like.

'I thought your grandmother might have put it here. She's the one everyone calls a witch, isn't she? I'd like to meet her.'

'You can't,' said Ella. 'She's sick. And she's *not* a witch.'

'Hey, hey, calm down,' he said. He looked panicked suddenly, as if he realised she was done talking to him.

Magpie was calmer now, and Ella gave her her head and flicked her seat to start her moving. 'Well, see you.'

Magpie stepped eagerly; she couldn't wait to get away.

'Wait, don't go.' He tried to step in Magpie's path, but the pony flattened her ears and threw her head up, ready to strike him again.

'Sorry,' said Ella. 'I told you, I have to get going.'

Gus raised his two palms and took a step back, defeated. 'Aye, all right then. I get it.' He reached up a hand and rubbed his hat against his head, as if scratching an itch.

Ella and Magpie crossed the road and took the bridle path to the lake. Ella was aware of Gus staring at her back, unmoving, but she put him out of her mind. She wasn't going to let him ruin her morning ride.

Here the path was wide and open, and with a click of her tongue she urged Magpie into a canter. Magpie needed no persuasion; she glided easily into the gait, smooth as cream. The lake came closer, a silver and pink jewel reflecting the sky — a cloud mirror. Ella drove her heels down and moved her body with the canter, girl and horse in perfect rhythm and synchronicity. She lost herself in the gentle sound of Magpie's thrumming hooves and the feel of the chill wind on her face.

She hadn't really thought about where she would go to look for Josh. Instead, Magpie had carried her towards the lake and Ella had let her. She now knew exactly which part of the lake they were headed for: the quiet keld. Where the river met the lake, where they had found the mauled sheep, and where . . . yes, she had to think it . . . where her father had liked to fish.

Her mother carried so much guilt about what had happened, and it didn't help that the people in town seemed to blame her too. Morag tortured herself: if only she'd checked on him when he didn't come home, instead of assuming the fishing was slow, that he'd lost track of time waiting for them to start biting, as he often did. Really it was the peace and quiet he liked. Morag would sometimes have to go and get him, leaving the girls with Grizzly, jumping on Sir Ed and cantering down to the lake to let off some of the storm clouds in her head. They'd stand on the shore arguing until Will shrugged his shoulders and hopped on his quad bike to head for home.

But that day she was busy with the children, and the

horses, and she figured he'd come home for dinner. But he didn't. He didn't come home all night, and as soon as it was light she rode down the track to the lake, somehow knowing he wouldn't be there — and he wasn't. He'd run off and left her, or so she thought, but his quad bike was still there, and his rod and his tackle. Even the camping chair and his thermos half full of tea. The lake, normally so turquoise, was dark that day, a shadow of the black clouds overhead that threatened rain but never delivered.

They were approaching the keld now, and the air was darkening again, and Ella's head was full of her mother's pain. She'd overheard Morag telling Grizzly all of it; she wasn't supposed to hear. They had never held a funeral for him, because there had been no body to bury, and though her mother talked of him as though he were drowned, and the townspeople threw them accusing looks, Ella could not accept that he was not coming back, ever.

Suddenly, Magpie stopped. Ella slid over her shoulder and landed in a heap. It could have been much worse. She had kept hold of the reins and she was unhurt.

'Magpie!' she barked, picking herself up. 'What was that for?'

But Magpie wasn't looking at her. She wasn't hanging her head sheepishly like she used to do when she was younger and her antics left Ella on her bottom in the training ring. Instead, her head was held high. Her feet were planted wide, and gusts of air blew in and out of her nostrils. Her eyes were bright with danger.

Ella's first thought was that there were more dead sheep. Or worse: that something terrible had befallen Josh, and they had found him. She almost didn't want to turn and see what Magpie was looking at. But turn she did, and what she saw took her breath away. Together, girl and pony stood tall and gazed upon the wondrous sight in front of them.

Standing at the edge of the lake, no, *in* the lake, with water covering its fetlocks, was the largest, most magnificent creature Ella had ever seen.

12

A horse stood in the water, drinking. It was as black as
night, its sheen reflecting the colours of the streaked sky
and the dark, impenetrable water. The Ben had turned
grey, its shadowy shape mirrored in the lake, along with
fat, lustrous clouds.

There was power in the horse's limbs, in its solid body,
in its broad chest — Ella could sense it pulsing. It was
massive, a mountain, built for battle. Its long, untamed
mane and tail dripped with water, glossy green weeds
from the lake caught in its tangles.

'Hello there,' she called softly, not wanting to scare

it away, but something told her that this horse was not easily spooked.

It slowly raised its head, staring, its muzzle dripping. Ella froze. It was almost too perfect, like a painting of an idea of a horse rather than something real. She held her breath. There was no sound; even the undersong had died away, with no birds or distant sheep calling, no susurration of the tussock and shrubs. The horse tossed its head, sending droplets of water through the air, then picked up its feet and splashed leisurely through the shallows to stand on the stony beach. The keld was as smooth as steel in the lake beyond.

Behind Ella, Magpie's nervous call broke the stillness. The stallion lifted a hoof and pawed the ground, sending a spray of coarse sand behind. It rumbled a deep whinny in response, which radiated out from its body and echoed around the Basin. Ella felt its call. She dropped Magpie's reins and moved forward, unable to stop herself.

She left the path and crunched across the sand towards it. She was vaguely aware of her pony behind her, the state of her: anxious, her shoes catching a stone which rang out. Magpie gave an agitated grunt but did not follow.

The great horse waited for Ella to come to it. As she moved, her stomach lifted like a bird. She tried to think of a word for what she was looking at, what she was feeling, but nothing came to mind, not even one of Grizzly's words. If there is no word for something, is it real? If you can't name something, does it exist? This horse was outside language. It was outside this time and place; she knew it in her bones. It was of the earth but not of this place. It was made of memory, and fire, and water.

Closer she drew, until she stood in front of it, taking in the sheer size of it. This was an animal that could crush her under its hooves on a whim. But she felt no fear. She stood her ground and bowed her head. She sensed the horse stretching its head towards her, and then she felt its hot breath in her hair. It smelled oily and thick, of fish and spring grass, but also something darker, loamy, like toadstools. She raised her head and stared into its tawny eyes.

Her body flooded with light. She felt a force then, pulling her towards the horse's shoulder. Its back was way over her head, but she knew that if she just touched it, if she just leapt, she would soon be sitting on top of the world. Its mane hung like a curtain, well past its neck, and she could grab it and leap. She could already see the ride in her mind: the freedom she would feel, how the creature would spring away on taut muscles; how it would take her away, away from everything — from her sad family, from the unspeakable black hole of grief she had not allowed herself to fall into. Maybe, just maybe, it would take her to her father. She slowly reached out a hand, and for a moment she thought she saw her face, muffled, distorted, reflected in its coat — and hesitated.

The stillness and silence was pierced by a screech, and from the corner of Ella's eye came a missile — black and white, flapping wings. Ella snapped out of whatever state she had fallen into — a dream? — in time to see a magpie dive-bomb the horse. It swooped and then swerved away.

The stallion shook its head, irritated, and flicked its tail, as if to dislodge a persistent fly. The magpie came again, and this time it didn't swoop away. Its beak made contact with the horse's ears. It was soon joined by another, and the air around them was filled with their squawks. Ella put up a protective arm to shield herself, but it wasn't her the birds were after. She stumbled backward, and hit the hard ground with a painful bump.

More magpies came; they flapped around the horse's head, a maelstrom. The horse reared up onto its hind legs, and then it attacked. It opened its jaw wide, and Ella saw its terrible teeth, larger and sharper than a horse's teeth should be. It lunged at the birds, grabbing one and crunching, before tossing aside its lifeless body. Again and again, like bobbing for apples in a barrel, it went for them, and each time succeeded in ripping another bird out of the air and throwing its mangled body to where Ella sat, cowering now, on the shore. Among the birds, the stallion looked at her with shining eyes, and as it threw the bodies on the ground, it came closer and closer to where she sat.

She should get up, move, run away, but she couldn't. She closed her eyes. Any moment now the horse's enormous black hooves would come down on her. Through the blur of her lashes she thought she saw the shape of the beast change. Its glossy black hide was reflective, metallic, and its tail had thickened and now thrashed from side to side, knocking magpies away. Instinctively, she threw up her arm, a useless protection, and waited for impact.

Instead, she heard hooves from behind her and another sound, a high whinny edged with fear. Magpie. While her namesake birds lay smashed on the ground, Magpie the pony moved like lightning to stand between Ella and the stallion.

All went quiet.

The stallion spat out a last bird and the rest of the

magpie army retreated, flapping up into the sky to observe from a safe distance. Magpie reared up and was suspended there, tiny next to the bigger horse — a toy, or a carousel horse.

And with that, the spell was broken.

Ella saw the stallion falter, back away a step.

They had to get out of there. The horse would kill Magpie too, given the chance. She leapt to her feet. Magpie returned to earth and pawed the ground.

Ella knew what to do. She had never moved so fast in all her life. She sprang into the saddle and took up the reins. She went to turn Magpie's head for home, but the pony was already in motion. She wheeled around, kicking up sand, and reached the bridle path. Magpie's power gathered and broke beneath Ella like a storm as she took off at a gallop. The stallion screamed in rage, and then the thunder of Magpie's hooves filled Ella's head. She twisted in the saddle, expecting to see the stallion follow them — it would have caught them in seconds — but instead she saw an empty beach, ripples on the water, and the saddest sight of all, dead magpies strewn about while a cloud of their kin circled the keld like a mournful whirlwind.

* * *

ELLA MANAGED TO pull Magpie up to a walk as they reached their driveway; despite everything that had happened, and how frightened she'd been, she didn't want her mother's wrath on top of it. It had been drilled into her over and over about not galloping the horses in the direction of home, and about letting them cool down sufficiently. The sun had appeared in the sky now, the blue as washed-out as eggshells, diluted by a layer of high cloud.

Morag stood with her hands on her hips in the yard. She came forward and reached out to grab Magpie's bridle, but the pony snorted and backed away from her. Ella jumped off her back and stood holding her reins, a safe distance from her mother. Her legs trembled but her hands were steady. She braced herself for the blasting.

But Morag merely folded her arms and sighed. 'I'd prefer it if you stayed where I can see you at the moment, and especially not go down to the lake alone. Did you have a good ride?' Her voice was not as cold as Ella had expected. Could it be that she felt bad about yesterday? Taken aback, Ella just nodded, her cheeks flushing. How could she tell her about what had happened now? About the danger she had been in at the lake? About the horse and its sharp teeth and about Magpie rescuing her?

Magpie pulled her towards the drinking trough, and Ella rested her forehead on her hot, damp neck, trying to compose herself. A fine mist of steam rose from her pony's body, the only clue to the mortal danger they had been in.

She tried to make sense of what she had seen: the horse and its massive bulk, but also the trick of the light when its hide turned scaly and shining; when its tail had transformed to a serpent's and back again. The huge teeth. More images came to her: a glimpse of the horse lingering at the edge of the paddock near the other horses, who skittered in alarm; her dream; the torn bodies of sheep strewn across the paddock. She opened her eyes with a start and stared over Magpie's neck towards the lake. Surely not. A horse wouldn't kill a sheep, would it? Rip its head clean off? But those teeth . . . they were otherworldly.

And then there was the powerlessness she had felt at the feet of the horse. She had been emboldened to walk up to it, to nearly touch it even, and she'd had a strong urge to jump on its back. Despite its massive height, she felt confident that, had she jumped, some force would have carried her up there. Then who knows what would have happened to her? If the birds hadn't attacked, breaking the spell, and then Magpie hadn't intervened . . . Where would she be now? Would she have just . . . disappeared? Like . . . like Josh had?

She felt the breath leave her body and her legs almost give way beneath her. *Josh.* Gone. She had felt the pull of the horse. Could that be what had happened to him? And if so, *where was he now?*

'ELLA!'

Morag was standing behind her. Ella turned, trying to set her face to look calm again.

'Where were you?' Morag asked.

'What do you mean? I was just . . .'

'You were miles away — I was calling you. Can you hurry up please and put Magpie away. Make sure you rug her up well. Looks like you worked her quite hard and we don't want her getting cold while she's still damp. Come on, we've got a trek to get ready for.'

Ella felt her eyes grow wide. 'Not to the lake!'

Morag stopped and stared at her. 'No, as it happens. These ones want to go up the Ben and get the view. But what's wrong with the lake? It's fine if we're all together. I just didn't want you going there by yourself, not with Josh going missing.'

Ella said nothing.

'Ella.'

'It's nothing,' said Ella. 'The Ben is good.' She forced a weak smile.

'Look, I know you'd rather ride Magpie, but why don't you get on Duke today. He'll look after you. You'll be fine.'

Ella nodded and turned to lead Magpie to her hitching post. She rubbed her down and put her cover on, as her mother had instructed. As she led her back to the paddock, Magpie followed close behind her — too close. She didn't move when Ella took her halter off. Normally she would trot away, ears pricked, to see her friends, or get to a patch of dirt and lie down for a roll even if she was wearing her blanket. Instead, she stood with her head down. Ella put her hand on the crescent moon on her pony's forehead, and Magpie closed her eyes. They stood like that for a minute. They knew that something momentous had happened, that they had survived something maybe they shouldn't have, and it had strengthened their bond.

Magpie's tiny ears trembled and Ella found herself wondering about them again. She had accepted them as a quirk, and the vet had dismissed them as an unusual development, nothing to be concerned about. But now she saw them as a proud sign of difference, like the green hue of the black patches in Magpie's coat when the sun reflected off them.

There was no doubt about it: Magpie was special. A brave little horse who had protected her. Ella had a creeping feeling that Magpie had saved her life.

13

The party that day was a group of confident teenage girls
and their mothers. The two women were around Morag's
age, with wide grins, and the easy seats of people who'd
been around horses most of their lives and were rediscov-
ering them after a bit of a break.

Hana was leading as usual, but Morag had saddled up
Olive and would accompany them for some of the way.
'Just in the mood,' she said, but Ella wondered if she was
keeping an eye on her.

The line of horses made a snake up the slope below
the Ben, a curving line through the brown and golden

landscape. Ella took the rear, and with the sound of the wind in her ears she fell behind. The flitting of finches played in her peripheral vision and a single pipit kept her company, leaping from fencepost to shrub. She could almost pretend that things were normal.

Morag was trotting alongside the group, the only one allowed to break out of the line, assessing the riders' abilities.

'Ready for a bit more speed?' she called. A resounding 'yes' came from the group and they broke into a controlled canter. One or two riders whooped in delight. This was the open paddock where experienced riders could gather more speed. It had fewer rabbit holes than others, fewer surprises; a wide track rose gently with a gate at the far end where the horses knew to slow and stop. Duke needed no encouragement, and while the others went at a rocking-horse pace, he sped up, Ella forcing her heels down and feeling him stretching beneath her, the cool air nipping at her cheeks. She was soon coming up behind Morag, who put out a hand to wave her past. They drew parallel for a moment, mother and daughter, huge grins on their faces, before Morag slowed to let Ella into the line just as the front horses were coming up to the gate.

'That was fun!' said one of the younger girls, her cheeks pink. 'Can we go again on the way back?'

'Not on the way back,' said Hana. 'But there's another spot further on where we can have another go. It's got a great view of the lake too. Ella, can you open the gate for us?'

Ella nodded, and softly heeled Duke forward to stand parallel to the gate while she opened it. Duke knew the drill and barged against it. They went through, then turned to wait beside it while the other horses came through one at a time, led by Hana and tailed by Morag.

'Thanks, love,' said Morag, and for once she didn't make a comment on Ella's technique or point out what she had done wrong. 'I think I'll head back now — you and Hana seem to have things under control.' She smiled, but she still looked worried.

Of course we do, thought Ella. Morag wheeled around and set off at a trot towards home. She was the only one who was allowed to do that.

The riders continued at a fast walk, the horses picking up their feet, ears pricked in curiosity at the world around them. It was much livelier for them, thought Ella, with experienced riders. On some days they looked almost asleep. Plodding along. The canter would have pushed their blood around, reminded them they were alive. Ella knew how they felt. She lived for speed sometimes, to wake her up, feel adrenaline through her veins. It always put her in a good mood afterwards. She wondered if it helped Fi too, whether it lifted her out of her dark moods.

As they came around a corner on the narrow sheep track on the side of the Ben, the lake was spread out before them. Some of the riders slowed to fawn over it, but the horses must have sensed something was coming. They all stopped and refused to go on.

Ella felt it too. It came from the lake, like a shiver; a flickering in the air, similar to the shimmer of a mirage on a road on a hot day. The horses turned their faces towards it. Hana, at the front, was trying to urge Sir Ed on, but the big dun refused to move. She gave him a tap with her riding crop and he tossed his head but stayed where he was. It was hard to know if the other horses were similarly cragfast or if they were merely waiting for their leader to lead.

Underneath Ella, Duke began to tremble, and then she felt it — the sense you get when you stand near an open freezer. It was getting cold suddenly, but she was only near the cold, not inside it. A whisper. The shimmer from the lake had breached its shore and was edging up over the paddocks towards them.

Up the front, Hana's phone rang. Ella heard her voice, clipped, making its way down the line, but couldn't hear

141

what she was saying. Then Hana put the phone back in her pocket and turned Sir Ed's head for home. This time, the horse moved. Hana trotted back down past the five trekkers, and said, 'Please follow me.' When she got to where Ella and Duke were waiting, her mouth was a grim line.

'That was Morag on the phone. There's an unexpected cold front coming.' The shimmer. 'Like, a really bad one, and it's moving fast. We need to get the horses back and make room for them in the stables.' She twisted in her saddle and called out, 'Who's up for a trot?'

A couple of the riders raised their hands, and that was all the encouragement Hana needed. She urged Sir Ed away, and the other horses followed. One of the riders was smiling; the rest didn't look so sure.

Ella knew the situation was serious, because they weren't supposed to go fast on the way home, and trotting downhill was definitely not advised. But she supposed that as long as the horses were kept at a trot, zig-zagging down the track, and didn't canter, then they would continue to follow the leader and not bolt and try to race each other back.

Ella waited until the last rider had passed, then she brought up the rear. Her face was starting to freeze and her eyes water. Duke was grunting. As they neared the stables, she heard the riders calling to each other, and to Hana, 'Hey, where are we going? We haven't had an hour yet!' But it was as though Hana was deaf to their protests; on, on, she led them, towards home.

Only as they clattered around the yard did Hana finally address them. 'I'm so sorry. We have to cut the trek short. There's a cold front coming and the safety of the horses is paramount. We need to get them ready.'

One of the women, a freckled red-head, snorted. 'Couldn't you have waited half an hour? They're animals for goodness' sake! They're used to the elements. Look at their coats!' And she plucked at Rocky's fuzzy hide — she was right there. Ella wanted to know the answer to that as well. But Hana ignored her and vaulted off Sir Ed.

Morag had come out of the barn and was barking instructions. 'Both feet out of the stirrups before you dismount, please. Do you want to ruin my good saddle?'

The riders were glancing at each other, bewildered. The red-haired woman stayed where she was. She wasn't going to get off until she'd had an explanation. Finally Hana walked alongside her and looked up.

'I'm very sorry about this,' she said quietly. 'We will refund you half of your fee. It's this cold front. It's serious, and it's coming in fast.' Hana was agitated; her face was pleading.

'I saw the forecast,' said the woman. 'It's supposed to be a beautiful spring day.' But even as she spoke, Ella saw that she shivered suddenly and let go of the reins to pull her jacket tighter.

Morag wasn't having any more of it. She marched up to Rocky and took the reins.

'Off,' she said. 'Now.' Her face said, *Don't mess with me.* Her white hair was flying about her face, her blue eyes stormy seas. Josh Underhill's voice came into Ella's head then: *Your mother's a witch, your gran's a witch, are you a witch?*

The woman clocked the look and nodded, a red patch flaring on her neck. She leaned forward and swung her leg over. She grunted as she landed heavily on her feet.

'This is bull,' she muttered, and stalked off towards her friends, shaking her long hair loose from her helmet, which she flung on the ground. The group was now huddled together against the cold, talking quietly, their hands jammed under their armpits and their breath starting to cloud in front of their faces. Ella set to work; she wasn't going to stop and question her mother. Morag had never been great with the customers, but after what had happened the day before, she would be careful not to upset them unless there was a real reason.

One of the riders had her phone out and gasped

loudly. The red-haired woman grabbed it off her and looked shocked as she glanced at the screen. She gave it back, and walked over to where Morag and Hana were busy rubbing down and rugging up the horses.

'I've just seen it. I'm really sorry for the way I reacted. You're absolutely right.'

Morag nodded an acknowledgement and gave a tight-lipped 'Thanks.'

The woman stood there for a moment, as if unsure what to do next. 'Can we . . . can we help?'

Morag and Hana looked at each other, but Morag shook her head.

'Thanks,' said Hana, 'but we really need you all out of the way . . . unless . . .' She turned to Morag. 'They could bring the other horses in?'

Morag sighed. She looked as though she knew she didn't have a choice. 'Okay. One horse per person, though. *Not* Magpie. Ella will have to go with them. Ella! Take the halters and go and bring the other horses in. These folk are going to help.'

It must be serious, thought Ella.

They set out to catch the remaining horses, Magpie, Olive, Peedie and Jubilee. Two of the teenagers looked like they would rather shovel doofers than catch horses, they were scowling so hard. Then one of them stumbled and put her hand down in a pile of dung, yelling a swear word as she landed. Soon the two of them were in fits of giggles, fooling about and lying on the ground, laughing.

The red-haired woman was walking next to Ella. 'Sorry about them,' she said, and peeled away to tell them off.

Ella was thankful the horses had decided to behave; some days they liked to trot away, keeping just out of reach while they casually ate grass. Magpie didn't need any persuading. As soon as she saw Ella coming, she picked her feet up and walked nimbly towards her, small ears pricked. She accepted the piece of carrot with a nudge. It was starting to get really cold now. Magpie had steam rising from her nostrils as she breathed, giving her the appearance of a fire-breathing dragon, but at least she was already rugged, as were the others. With Magpie in hand, Ella turned to help get halters on. Despite freezing fingers the job was done and they led the horses back through the main gate and into the yard.

The barn doubled as extra stables for emergencies, with makeshift stalls. Morag and Hana had driven the quad bikes out to make room, and covered them with tarpaulin. Half the horses were already settled inside. Now the women were spreading straw around in thick layers so the horses could lie down, and making sure their spaces were hazard free. They managed to rope the guests in to spreading out the straw, and the teenage girls cheered up a bit as they moved out of the cold, throwing straw at each other as they went.

With a last check that the horses were rugged up, they turned on the heaters and closed the stable doors. The horses were all happily eating from their hay nets: all except Magpie, whose head was held high, staring after Ella. She whinnied as they shut the doors.

Outside, the air cut like a knife. The trekkers rushed for their cars and drove away, no doubt with the heaters blasting. There was a rumble over the lake. Thick black clouds were creeping towards them, fat and lush with snow.

'Come on,' said Morag. 'Inside. You too, Hana. We'll make up the spare bed. I could use your help overnight if anything happens with the horses.' It wasn't a question.

Hana nodded anyway. 'Just let me call Mum. She'll be expecting me to help at home, but she'll understand. She's got enough hands, I think.'

'Thanks,' said Morag. 'Sometimes I wish I had an army of sons like your mum does. But I'm grateful for you.' She squeezed Hana's arm.

Flames were leaping high in the log burner, crackling a warm welcome, when they came into the house. Grizzly and Fiona were side by side at the picture window, a blanket draped over their shoulders, staring out towards the lake. Ella went over to stand beside them. She thought she saw a dark shape moving in the distance.

Then Grizzly spoke. Her voice was low and broken. 'Something is coming, bairns, and I don't like it.'

Fiona, beside her, piped up. 'It's already here, Grizzly.' She turned and looked at Ella, who could do nothing but nod and swallow the giant lump in her throat.

THEY KEPT THE fire lit and ran all the heaters — until the power failed. Morag dragged all their mattresses into the living room and they slept there, blankets piled high, with Morag, Hana and Ella taking turns to wake up and put more wood in the burner. Morag was most concerned about Grizzly, who was so weak now and her skin so thin. She felt every granule of cold air that slipped through. She slept with a woollen hat on, and when Ella woke in the night she could see Grizzly's eyes shining black in the flickering firelight. Sometimes she heard her whispering to herself in words she didn't understand. Fiona slept curled up like a puppy against her mother.

When Ella woke the next morning, the first light radiated blue around the curtains. The world had turned white overnight. Morag told her to stay in bed, where it was warmer, and left the others sleeping while she bustled around, pulling on layers of clothes to go and check on the horses.

As she came back, stamping her boots on the front doorstep, and unwrapping the scarf from around her face where only her eyes had been showing, the lights flickered back on at last.

'Are they all right?' asked Ella, rubbing sleep from her eyes.

'They will be once we've got some hot mash inside them. The heating failed there too, and they're a bit stiff and slow, so we were right to rug them up as much as we did. And it's certainly warmer in the stables than it is outside.' She removed her gloves and crossed over to the kitchen. 'I just need to check . . .' She turned on the tap and there was a groaning sound from deep in the house. 'As I thought. The pipes are frozen.' She turned on the battery-powered radio and opened the pantry. She disappeared inside, and emerged a moment later dragging a huge plastic bottle of water with a tap at the bottom of it.

'Here,' said Hana. 'Let me help.'

Together they hoisted it onto the bench.

'We'll have to use this sparingly,' said Morag. 'Hana, can you go and check the horses' water? Break the ice if you have to. Take my coat.'

Hana nodded, and spent a long time piling enough clothes on to keep warm before going outside. The icy air wafted in like a cold finger on their necks.

The warbling music on the radio ceased and seven pips marked the hour. The newsreader announced unprecedented low temperatures in the Basin, minus 20 degrees. There were reports of dead chickens and sheep, of electricity cut off and frozen pipes. Birds had dropped from the sky, especially magpies. Ella felt the cold travel down her back, and shook it off.

She went to the window and looked out. The sky was a lumpen grey, the earth a dirty white from a thin layer of snow and ice. The horses' paddock was stark and empty, and dotted with small dark shapes. Magpies. She felt a prickling in her sinuses, a sudden spring of hot tears. She looked the other way, across the drive and down to the lake. What was usually a bright turquoise blue was today a menacing black. It was as though a cold, malignant spirit had rolled over the valley, coming off the lake and turning it dark.

It felt like a punishment.

The shape of the Ben, now capped white, was draped in a thick scarf of cloud around its base.

And suddenly, out of nowhere — a black horse, standing in the paddock that a moment ago had been empty. Looking at her. A high whinny escaped and reverberated across the valley.

Morag strode to the window, and even Grizzly, from her spot on the couch, under blankets, looked up, alarmed.

'What the devil was that?' said Morag, and she gently pushed Ella to one side and opened the curtain further. 'How did that get there? Whose horse is that? Ella? Do you know? Is that the one you saw the other day?'

Ella just nodded, a cold lump in her throat.

'Well, that's the one in my dream the other night. I've never seen it before for real. It must be freezing.' Even from here they could see clouds of mist from its nostrils. 'Why is it just standing there? Can it see us?'

Then Grizzly was there, by their side. Ella was surprised at how tiny she seemed, wrapped in her blanket, her woollen hat still jammed on her head. She reached out a thin hand to pull back the curtain.

'*Holy crivvens!* It can't be,' she whispered. And then she was down, sunk to her knees. Ella managed to catch her before she toppled further.

'Grizzly!' Fiona exclaimed, and rushed over.

Morag picked her up and carried her to the couch. Grizzly's eyelids flickered and she moaned. Then her eyes were fully open as she laid her head back on a fresh pillow. She gripped Morag by the wrist. 'What have I done?' she said. 'It's all making sense. I'm so sorry.' And before they could ask her what she meant, she closed her eyes again, in sleep or a faint, it was impossible to tell.

'Should we call an ambulance?' asked Fiona, crying soft, silent tears.

'She's just fainted, love. It's probably the shock of the cold. I'll call the clinic. I'm not sure how anyone will get around — the road will be treacherous, all that ice and snow. What did she mean? Does anyone know what she meant?'

Ella looked at her grandmother, sleeping almost peacefully, so small in her blanket, so grey and papery. Grizzly used to be strong, browned by the sun and wind, with creases in her face from smiling and squinting into the bright days. She trained and rode the horses, mucking out, lifting hay bales with her tanned, wiry forearms bulging. She always used to wear a battered straw hat that had belonged to her husband, its rim coming away from the top of it. Since she got cancer, she hadn't worn it as much, and now she needed a hat to ward off the cold, not the heat.

While Morag was on the phone, waiting for someone to answer, Grizzly opened her eyes again. She saw Ella and Fiona gathered around her, concern ruffling their faces, and sighed. She extracted her hands from under the blanket and took theirs, one in each.

'My lovelies,' she said. 'I was having the strangest dream.'

'Are you all right, Grizzly?' asked Fiona. 'We're worried about you.'

'Yes, lass, I am fine, just having a little sleep, that's all.'

'You fainted, Mum,' said Morag. 'I'm calling the clinic now.'

'Ach, I'm *fine*, I said.' This was no-nonsense Grizzly. The Grizzly who had worked through her pain before finally going to the doctor and finding out she had cancer.

Morag ignored her and stayed on the phone. Finally someone answered and Morag turned her back on them and walked into the kitchen, murmuring no doubt so Grizzly wouldn't hear the fear in her voice.

Grizzly squeezed the girls' hands.

'What did you mean,' said Ella, 'when you said you were sorry? About what?'

Grizzly closed her eyes for a moment, and when she opened them again they were rimmed with moisture. She let out a breath of air through pursed lips. She didn't look at them.

'It was the horse,' she said. 'The horse made it all make

sense. I should have known with that dream. And your Magpie. The signs were there but I didn't want to see.'

'Signs?' said Ella.

'It was her ears. Those funny little ears. Something so tiny, so insignificant, but it's her coat as well. I've seen how it looks green in the light. Like an oil slick. Or liquorice. You know. And then my Bobby, the lake. Your dad. Oh.' Her face was stricken.

Ella just felt confused, and probably looked it too, because Grizzly's eyebrows went up and she nodded. 'I'll start at the beginning.'

14

An toiseach: the beginning
Braw: handsome

Griselda grew up on a croft near a loch in the Highlands of Scotland. The whole family toiled the farm and at the end of the day, their bones weary, came together for dinner in the cosy kitchen where they ate and laughed and sometimes sang songs. Griselda had black hair, and broad shoulders from lifting hay bales and milking cows. She loved her work; she sang to the cows to help bring their milk in, and she loved the feeling of her muscles taut beneath her skin.

One day, she was walking down by the loch with her little terrier Sookie. Sookie set up a terrible barking, and she crouched down to call the dog to her.

'What is it, wee one?' she asked.

A young man stood beside the loch, looking at her. His trousers were worn and held up by string, and buttons were missing on his shirt, causing it to fall open so his chest was exposed. He had black hair and black eyes with a mischievous glint that was just for her.

Griselda had met boys before. They usually teased her. Her ma told her that the more they teased her, the more it meant they liked her, but Griselda thought, *If that's how they treat me when they like me, I'd never want to be with them when we get into an argument.* No, she didn't need those filthy boys. She was quite happy on her own.

But this boy was different. He smiled at her, and she smiled back.

'Hello!' she said. 'Are you lost? Are you looking for the McGregor farm?'

'Yes,' said the boy. His voice was deep and still, like the pool in the nearby river.

'I'll show you if you like? It's not far.'

And so they walked. Their legs made sweeping sounds through the long grass. Sookie at first yapped and ran circles around them, even growled at the boy a bit, but he said a couple of soft words under his breath to her and she lay down and flopped, showing him her belly, asking for rubs.

Griselda chuckled. 'So fierce, she is. Look out or she'll attack you with her soft wee belly.'

The boy laughed and tossed his hair out of his eyes. It was then that she noticed the weeds in his hair, blending in with the dark strands, giving it a greenish tinge. She reached over to pull one out, but as she grasped and tugged he wrenched his head, and the weed, away.

'Your hair,' she said. 'It's full of weeds. I was only going to pull one out.'

'Leave it,' he said. 'I like it there.'

She laughed a bonny laugh. But she puzzled over him as well: the weed had not budged in her hand. It was as though it was a part of him.

When they reached the boundary between her family croft and Mr McGregor's, she stopped and watched the boy climb over the low drystone wall. 'What are you doing there?' she asked.

'Oh, I do whatever is needed,' he said, and took her hand. 'You're a lovely girl,' he said. 'Will I see you again?'

They arranged to meet again the next day.

At home, her mother commented on the roses in Griselda's cheeks and the lilt in her step. 'What's got into you, young lass? You been drinking the cream from the milking pot?'

Griselda only smiled a quiet smile and got on with her work. The mutton wasn't going to cook itself.

'What's your name?' she asked the boy when she saw him again.

'Aonghas Donn,' he replied. 'And yours?'

She told him her name and he repeated it several times, his voice getting ever more musical, like an incantation. Each time he said her name, the light changed, and he became more and more beautiful. A soft glow hung in the air around him.

She didn't pull away when he took her hand. His hands were rough, from work she supposed — her own were not exactly milky, though she rubbed them in the freshly shorn sheep's wool for the lanolin. She talked about her life, told him everything there was to know, including near-drowning when she was a girl, though it hadn't made her afraid — if anything, it made her more determined to swim in the loch, to dive into its black depths in search of the bottom. She could hold her breath for minutes at a time, thanks to the practice every summer since she was a wee bairn. She always carried her knife strapped to her leg when she swam now, since it was nothing more sinister than the weeds in the loch that had grabbed her and tried to hold her under. The same weeds that perpetually crowned the head of Aonghas Donn.

SHE BROUGHT HIM home one day to meet her family, but they didn't take to him at all. He *skulked*, her mother said. He seemed *sleekit* — crafty. He refused her offer of shortbread, only drank water furiously and eyed with hunger the pheasant hanging in the cool kitchen. He evaded questions about his family and only gestured towards the loch when they asked where his people were from. He laughed when Griselda's little sister Cait knocked her head on the table and cried. By the time the visit was up, an uncomfortable silence had fallen in the room and the only sound was the crackle of the fire in the stove and the ticking of the clock on the wall.

Griselda walked Aonghas out to the gate, feeling the shine go from the day and from the two of them. 'My family is everything to me,' she said. 'You disrespected them.'

'Ach,' said Aonghas, grabbing her hand. 'We don't need them. You're bonny and I'm braw and strong — what do we want their approval for?'

She pulled her hand away. 'Cocky, aren't ye? You're not so handsome that I'd turn my back on them, you know. There are plenty more hard-working boys in the village who like me just as much as you do.' She didn't say that she didn't like any of them back, but he had annoyed her.

He stopped at the gate and turned to face her. A shadow passed over his face, and to her surprise he had tears in his eyes. 'I'm sorry,' he said. 'I will be better. I will make sure your family can have no objection to me, you'll see.' A tear spilled down his cheek.

'You're crying,' she stated unnecessarily, for he was surely aware of his own tears.

'Wipe it away for me, my love,' he whispered. 'Please.'

She raised her hand and gently wiped the tear from his cheek, and as she did so she was flooded with warmth, and a vision came to her of the two of them, their future selves, laughing by the fire in the croft house, and she was dandling a bairn on her lap, and he was so handsome and strong she never needed to want for anything in life again.

'I love you,' she said, and Aonghas smiled.

'And I you, my love, and we will never let anyone come between us.'

They kissed and then he was gone, with a promise to meet her again tomorrow. She missed him already.

THE NEXT DAY SHE was working in the fields, dreaming of Aonghas, when her mother came to see her, dragging Cait with her.

'Griselda, love, I've just been over at the McGregors' croft with some eggs. Mrs McGregor has never heard of your Aonghas. He hasn't been working there at all. What's he up to? I'm worried, dearie.'

'She must be mistaken,' Griselda said. 'I'm sure she doesn't know everything that goes on there.'

Her mother sighed and walked away, shaking her head and threatening to talk to Griselda's father about it.

Griselda didn't care. She had Aonghas to meet that day and nobody was going to stop her. She threw off her work clothes, put on her floral frock, and set off down to the loch to meet him.

Aonghas was furious when he heard her mother had been asking about him. He called her all sorts of terrible names, and in her heart Griselda knew she didn't like it, but he was so braw and so strong that she forgave him straight away.

'I'll come tomorrow,' Aonghas said. 'I'll tell your father that I'm taking you away from this place and we will be married.'

'But where will we live?'

'Nearby,' he replied. 'Don't you worry. It's not important now. What will you be doing tomorrow at dinner time?'

'I'll be at home, after helping Da with the lambs.'

'Stay in the fields a while,' he said, 'and let me talk to them. It'll be better if you're not there.'

She thought it strange but she didn't question him. He knew what he was doing, and he was handsome and strong.

THAT EVENING, she decided she had waited in the fields long enough. She whistled to Sookie, who stopped chasing rabbits and leapt along beside her as she daundered through the tall grass. There was no sound but the swish swish of her sturdy legs and the panting of her dog.

As she approached the croft house, she saw a fire on the distant hill and stopped. She gasped. It wasn't a fire — it was the full moon, rising like a ball of flame to the east. It was enormous, and the reflection from the recently descended sun lit it up like nothing she had ever seen before. She stopped to stare at it and to marvel at the beauty of the world and everything in it. How perfect life was, in that moment.

But something was off. As she stood, there was only the sound of little Sookie still panting gently at her feet. The undersong had gone quiet. At this time of the evening there should have been birdsong carrying on the breeze — the whistling of a skylark and the trilling of the finches that usually flitted about and burst from the undergrowth when she passed. There was always the lowing of a bull, or a sheep; a dog barking in the distance. And any number of mechanical sounds as her father and the farmhands brought the machines in for the night, calling insults to each other and laughing as they finished the day, eager for a cold drink and a warm meal in their bellies.

Instead, there was silence. It was unsettling despite her bliss. She kept on walking, and reached the gate to the croft house. All of a sudden, a black shape exploded around the side of it. Griselda cried out in shock. A huge black horse, with a long dripping wet mane and a proud tail, skidded to a stop in front of her and then wheeled around. It clattered over the cobblestones of the path, through the vegetable garden, and leapt over the high stone wall — an impossible sight. On its back, her mother, her father, and little Cait clinging on for dear life to her mother's blouse.

Sookie started barking, a frenzied yapping that entered Griselda's befuddled brain, so she couldn't think, couldn't fathom what she'd just seen. She sat with a bump on the ground and waited.

Darkness fell around her, and soon the last call of the birds started up and the night sounds surrounded her. Stricken animals called to each other, and she was startled by the hoot and beating wings of an owl. She picked herself up and went inside the house, where the table was laid for dinner and a stew was bubbling its head off on the stove. A half-drunk glass of beer sat beside her father's favourite chair, and Cait's train set lay half assembled on the rug. But there was no sign of her family — they had simply vanished. And now she thought she must have imagined the horse, and her family on its back, because it made no sense to her at all, and so she decided it must have been a dream.

Later that night, he came to her. His hair and his clothes were wet, and water dripped from the weeds in his hair.

'Now we can be together, my love,' he said.

But the glow that had surrounded him was gone. The spell was broken. She saw him for what he was. His skin was sallow with a greenish tinge to it, and the weeds in his hair were slimy. They writhed as he walked towards her, holding out his hands. She backed away but he grabbed a hold of her.

'Come away now, my love, my bonny lass.'

'No!' she cried, but he had a hold of her left hand, and it was cold and clammy and she was stuck like glue to him. She grabbed for the first thing she could — a set of old horse brasses once worn by working Clydesdales that now hung on a leather strap by the fireside. She tore them off the wall and struck him across the face. He yelled and dropped her hand, stunned. She took her chance and ran for the door, and out into the garden. He stumbled after her, his hand on his cheek. She turned as she ran and saw his hand fall away, and the impression of the horse brass imprinted on his cheek, as though he had been branded with a hot iron. Then a horrible noise escaped from him and he began to change; a black shape, like a great dark shadow, engulfed him. Griselda didn't wait anymore. She grabbed the iron shears by the door, where her father had dropped them that afternoon, and flew through the gate with a shadow at her heels — Sookie. And as she ran, she heard hoofbeats. By the rowan at the end of the path, she turned to face them, brandishing the shears. The giant black horse sailed over the gate and clattered to a halt in front of her. Then it wheeled around and galloped for the loch.

'AND THAT WAS IT,' said Grizzly. 'I got myself a passport and I went as far away as I could. I knew that my family was gone, and there was nothing there for me, just danger.'

'And you never told anyone?' said Ella.

'Ach, who would believe me? I came to this country and I worked on farms. Then there was the country dance, the one where all the young menfolk hope to meet the love of their lives, preferably one who knows her way around a farm, and that was it. I met my Bobby. He wasn't handsome or particularly strong, but he was a hard worker, and he was kind, and he loved me something fierce. And I loved him too, in a steady way, not in a flighty, fluttering way. I was happy to settle here — it reminds me of home with its loch and its stark hills and craggy mountains. And we built this house here because I loved being near the loch and the views of the snowy ranges. But I also loved the natural ring of stones and that stone church on the hill. It all reminded me of home.

'I knew I'd never go back. I didn't need to. But I kept that place alive in my heart, and that's why I've taught you all those nature words, and your mother before you. And when Morag came along I knew this was my home, with her and Bobby, but after that we lost him, drowned in the lake. I warned him that the Nor'wester was coming through, but he wouldn't listen. If it wasn't for Morag and this farm, which needed seeing to, I wouldn't have made it through.

'Then along came you two, the absolute lights of my life.'

'But the horse . . .'

'A kelpie. Aonghas Donn was a kelpie through and through. A water horse. He bewitched me twice — the first was when he said my name, which got me on his hook, and the second time when he asked me to wipe that tear from his cheek. It bound me to him. He never meant for me to see him in his horse form until we were married. I saw him, and it broke the spell. Otherwise I'd have never got away.'

Ella thought for a moment, and didn't want to say it — but Fiona beat her to it. 'That horse? That black one, out there. Is it a kelpie? Did it take Josh Underhill?'

Grizzly closed her eyes, then opened them, and they could see they were filled with tears. Grizzly never cried, not that they had ever seen. Just as nearly drowning had made her less afraid of the water, losing all those she loved had made her less inclined to being sad about anything else. Nothing much could touch her anymore.

'I believe it is,' she said. 'And I don't think it is just any kelpie. I think it is Aonghas Donn come here to punish me for leaving him.'

'But how did it get here? And why take Josh?' asked Ella.

'I don't know why it would bother itself with a lad like that, but kelpies are spiteful creatures. Maybe young Josh slighted it somehow. I don't know. And as for how it got here — well, kelpies are not of our world. They move through the spirit realm, through the realm of the faeries. There are some places, liminal places, thin places, where they can pass through from one world to the next. Sometimes those places are full of magic and wonder and sometimes they are full of death and danger.

'When I got here, I was always feart it would follow me here, but I didn't know if it could. I planted that rowan tree by the gate as a protection. I didn't think there were kelpies in this country — why would there be? So it was only a precaution. I didn't know the birds were going to carry those seeds all over the land, but the more rowans that sprouted up by the lake, and by the river, the safer I felt. Then, about eight years ago, the district council announced that they were a noxious weed — never mind that the birds liked them, even the native ones. The rowans were smothering local plants, taking hold in the tussock. So they set about removing them everywhere. Fair enough, I suppose.'

'But we still have a rowan tree,' said Fiona. 'By the gate.'

'Aye, and I've been meaning to have it cut down all

this time, but I just couldn't bring myself to. I was always brought up with a rowan at the gate, to protect against things that want to cause us harm. But it didn't protect my family back in Scotland, did it? So maybe I'm just an old fool.'

'So there's no more rowan by the lake?' asked Ella.

'They took them all out, aye. I always felt safe with them there, but now they're gone, and I believe the kelpie has come to find me. You know what they say about families and curses, about tragedy — that they are doomed to repeat it. I've been waiting all this time, and now he's here.'

There was a clatter from the kitchen as Morag dropped a spoon in the sink. She was off the phone to the clinic. Now she raised her voice.

'Oh for god's sake, Mum. You're terrifying the children. Why don't you tell them the truth? That your family drowned in that lake. That a freak wave took them from the shore. That's what you said.'

'Aye, that's what I said. But it wasn't true. I only said it to protect you, love. Losing Bobby may have been a coincidence. I'll never know. But your man Will, just disappearing like that—'

'Stop. I talked to the doctor and he said as long as you're awake and talking you're fine, but I've half a mind to call him back and tell him you're delirious. That you're going downhill.'

Grizzly ignored her. 'He's punishing me, and he'll keep punishing us until he gets what he wants or we can stop him.'

'Enough.' Morag came over and took Fiona by the hand. 'Come on, love, let's go and get you dressed.' She pulled Fiona gently towards the stairs, but Fiona hung back, a dead weight, wanting to hear more. Her face was curious, her eyes alight, not terrified as Morag had decided. But she was no match for her mother's strength and soon they disappeared up the stairs.

'That Magpie of yours, Ellie. I didn't want to believe it, but it's in her ears. Those strange little ears — a sign of the kelpie's offspring. That poor mare had no choice. A kelpie decides what it wants and it takes it. No creature can resist it, not children, horses or women. So promise me, if you ever see a handsome stranger with weeds in his hair, you turn and run, you hear? And if you see that black horse, don't go near it.'

Ella knew that she should tell Grizzly what had happened with the horse by the lake — even though it could have just as easily been a dream — but she couldn't. It was as though the words escaped from her tongue every time she tried to summon them. As though

170

she had no control over them. She thought about brave Magpie, and how she had stood between her and the kelpie. No ordinary pony. There was something else, too. *If you ever see a handsome stranger . . .* Ella felt sick to her stomach, but she couldn't think why.

'What is it?' asked Grizzly. 'You look pained.'

She still couldn't get the words out, so she changed tack. 'You think the kelpie took Dad? Drowned him in the lake?'

'I don't know, my lovely, and that's the truth. But like I said, it feels to me like he is punishing me, punishing us, by taking the menfolk from us. And now there's none left, he'll find some other way to punish me.'

'And Josh?' She thought of the dream, of Josh, dripping wet — her feeling that he was gone. Was the kelpie showing them something?

'I don't know, my love. That, I don't know. It's a puzzle. But I'm afraid that Josh has gone the way of my family.'

15

The unwelcome snow lay on the ground for two days before a warmer sun appeared and the ungiving began — the cold snap relinquishing its grip on the land.

But before that, there was work to be done. The horses' paddock was littered with carcasses of frozen magpies. They couldn't leave them to thaw and rot — apart from anything else, they were a health hazard for the horses. Morag told Ella to push the wheelbarrow while she picked up bird after bird with a shovel, each one adding to the weight in the barrow, and in Ella's chest. They worked with thick gloves and socks on under their boots, but still the sharp cold bled into their skin and their breath made clouds in the air.

They tried to dig a hole but the ground was too hard and frozen, so they put them in two rubbish sacks and stored them behind the stables. There was something so forlorn about the magpie bodies, all piled together, rolling around in their sacks. When Morag wasn't paying attention, Ella said a quiet thanks to them for keeping watch over her; for distracting the kelpie and giving her the chance to break its hold over her.

When Morag had first opened the stable, she had found seven magpies roosting in the rafters: they must have snuck in to escape the cold. She tried to shoo them out, but they stayed resolute, and in the end she shrugged and let them stay, admiring their tenacity. Ella didn't know how much they understood about what had happened to their friends, but she hid the sacks from them and thought she detected a melancholy in their murmuring as they sidled along the wooden beams, watching her.

There were moments of beauty in the bleakness. The snow was dirty and grey — this was no winter wonderland — but Grizzly introduced the girls to all the words she knew for the glassy icicles that had hung from the roof and from the fences and that were now melting like tears. They repeated them, like mantras, as they went about feeding the horses in the stables. Fiona said they would make good names for horses:

ickle

shuckle

clinkerbell

daggler

tankle

shockle

aquabob

snipe

BY FRIDAY, THE snow had mostly gone from the ground, and a warmer breeze blew from the north. As Ella dressed in jodhpurs and a polar-fleece jacket, she gazed out the window at the empty paddock. They would let the horses out today. She remembered the dream she'd had the other night — how as well as seeing Josh, she'd seen the black horse cantering around and around, as if herding the horses. For a moment she forgot it was a dream and wondered what its plan was — to get them to follow it into the lake and drown them? She had a vision of the horse cantering on water, while the others trailed behind, getting deeper and deeper into the lake until only their nostrils were visible, before they went under, leaving only ripples.

She shook it off — she didn't need her imagination magnifying her anxiety.

A trek was planned for late morning, but Morag said that Ella could skip it and take Magpie and go for an early ride; they were both going stir-crazy. She would stay away from the lake, but on a whim she picked up Fiona's talisman from where it hung off the mirror before she left her room. She pulled off the rowan sprig and dropped it into the pocket of her jacket, then looped the twine and put it over her head. The feather, bone and small stone sat coolly between her collarbones. It made her feel safe.

When she opened the stable doors, the restless animals turned expectantly, looking for freedom and food.

Magpie whickered softly and nudged her as she entered her stall.

'Hey, girl,' said Ella. 'I've missed you.'

Magpie pawed the ground, rustling the straw and lifting it like candy floss. Ella ran her hands down the sides of the pony's face, then stroked her forelock. Magpie closed her eyes sleepily, enjoying her touch.

'Is it true?' Ella whispered. 'Are you a kelpie too?' She touched Magpie's ears, which were furred with the remains of her winter coat. It must have tickled; the ears twitched. 'How can it be?'

She thought of Olive then, Magpie's mother, under the spell of the kelpie. What did it mean to have a shape-shifting creature like that for a sire? Magpie wasn't different from any other horse, was she? And she was loyal, not some wild, untameable magical . . . monster.

But while she was loyal to Ella, and wouldn't hurt Fiona, she could be downright hostile to other people. That wasn't unusual, though, was it? For a horse?

'Oh, Maggie,' she said. 'What am I going to do with you?'

Magpie answered by blowing on her hand and softly lipping it, searching for snacks. Ella gave her one last pat on the neck and clipped the lead rope to her halter.

'Sorry, guys,' she said as she led Magpie past the other horses. 'Mum and Hana will be along soon.'

Duke and Joey banged on their stall doors. They thought she should be helping.

She led Magpie to her spot where she'd left an armful of hay. But instead of falling on it like she usually did, Magpie's ears went back and she danced restlessly on her feet.

Gus was standing in the yard, waiting. Ella was happy to see him, though she felt as though there was something she had forgotten about him; something she should be keeping in mind. Instead, she smiled.

'What about that cold?' he said, by way of greeting. He said it with his chest puffed out, as though he was proud.

'Yeah,' said Ella. 'The poor magpies.'

Gus flicked his head. 'It didn't get that one, I see.'

Ella looked. A lone magpie sat on the old pine stump beyond the stable, watching them.

'One for sorrow,' she said.

'What's that?'

'Nothing. What's up?'

'I thought we could have another ride today — what do you think? They haven't found the boy, I heard.'

Ella was doubtful they would find him. Not after the cold. Not alive anyway. She shivered.

'Sounds good,' was all she said.

'Do you have to ride Magpie?' he asked. 'Couldn't you ride someone else? You know she doesn't like me. I thought I could change her mind, or at least . . .'

'At least what?' said Ella.

Before he could answer, Morag came into the yard. 'Gus!' she said. 'How nice to see you. Have you come for a ride?'

'If that's all right with you,' he said, with forced politeness.

'Tell you what,' she said. 'You can have Storm again, but Ella, I'd like you to take Fiona with you. She can ride Peedie. Grizzly's in bed and Rita's coming to look after her, but Fiona needs some fresh air. No, don't look at me like that! She's getting pretty good. She can trot and canter with confidence. Okay?'

'Ugh, *fine*,' said Ella.

'so you're the famous sister,' said Gus, as Fiona emerged in the yard. She wore her yellow raincoat and chunky ankle-length riding boots. Her face was solemn and she nodded at him, but put Peedie between them and leaned into the pony's shaggy coat. She brushed him quickly, then spent a long time combing his bushy mane. She liked to plait it and weave feathers and ribbons into it. Every now and then she watched Gus silently over Peedie's neck.

As they were finishing getting the ponies ready, Hana arrived, sporting a new short haircut. One side had been shaved almost to bare skin, exposing the row of rings that travelled around her ears. As usual she looked immaculate, with clean, tight jodhpurs, electric pink this time, and a plaid vest. Her style gave the customers confidence in her, she always said, made her look like she knew what she was doing. Ella thought it also lent her a sense of fun, which made others relax.

'Who's your friend?' Hana asked, smiling kindly — a genuine smile. She was holding a big pot in both hands.

Gus nodded at her, averting his eyes, and finished tightening Storm's girth before moving to his head and murmuring in his ear, smoothing the horse's forelock over the browband of his bridle.

'That's Gus,' said Ella.

'Why do you even use these bridles?' Gus said suddenly. 'Nasty, horrible cold bits in their mouths. They'd let you ride them without, you know. And saddles. So uncomfortable.'

Hana laughed. 'What a character you've found, Ellie! Where's Morag? Mum's made her a casserole. Thought she might not have had a chance to go shopping with the snow and stuff.'

'She's in the stable,' said Ella.

'Have fun!' Hana said as she strode away.

'I do ride Magpie without a saddle and bridle some-times,' Ella said to Gus. She was suddenly anxious to impress him. 'But we don't go outside the paddock. Mum would never let us.'

Gus shrugged, but his face told her he thought that was stupid. Which made Ella mad, because she couldn't articulate something that just *was*. It was just how things were done.

By the time their mounts were ready, the sun was climbing in the sky, and the patches of snow on the Ben were mimicked by the shadows of the sparse clouds that moved across them, driven by a warm, twitchy wind that tugged at their clothes and tossed the horses' manes. The horses were twitchy too — after being cooped up for so many days they were eager to let off some energy.

Ella stayed close to Peedie and Fiona, keeping an eye on them. The Shetland pony strutted with his head high like he was on the runway, tossing his long black forelock out of his eyes. Fifi stared intently ahead of her, reins in both hands, and every now and then, when Peedie couldn't help but give a joyous wee buck, she gripped his mane. Her lips moved, and Ella was unsure whether she was talking to Peedie or to herself, to remind herself to keep her heels down, moving with the rocking motion of her pony, to keep her hands down but not to grab the saddle unless strictly necessary. Her yellow coat was a beacon against the golden tussock, and her white hair flew from under her black helmet. If she was scared, or worried, she was doing a good job of talking herself out of it.

Gus was impatient, and rode circles around the girls, laughing, as though in love with the guttural wind and the fresh spring air, in love with life. He whooped, tipping his head back, his dark eyes blinking at the sun.

'Come on, girls,' he urged. 'Life is beautiful!'

Fiona looked at Ella and rolled her eyes. She'd been watching him, evaluating him, and he'd come up wanting, it seemed.

The ground was boggy from the extreme weather, and after a burst of cantering which threw half-moon divots of mud in the air, and one or two onto their clothes, they slowed to a walk at the top of the incline. Snow lingered in the dips and shadows of the hill. The lake spread out below them, and in the distance the mountains were bright white. A hawk hung, aloof, in the air above them.

Once again they were by the church and the small graveyard. Ella took off her jacket; the day was warming up. Soon there'd be no snow left.

She thought about the last time she was here. What if Josh had been hiding in the church all this time? Had hidden when she came looking? She hadn't stayed long. Ella didn't remember hearing that it had been searched. What if he had escaped the kelpie or whatever he was running from, and was crouched between the pews?

She wondered what had happened to the black horse

and, with a shudder, what it might do next. Now, the perfect day, the warmth after the extreme cold, seemed like a trick. She had let herself forget for a moment the crushing worry of the past few days, the unearthly cold snap that had felt like a punishment for evading the kelpie that day. A cloud passed over the sun, its shadow moving up the Basin towards them.

Gus was looking at her strangely.

'What?'

'That thing around your neck. What's that supposed to be?'

Ella had forgotten the talisman, and grabbed it, holding it in her hand, hiding it from his prying eyes. 'It's nothing.'

He looked at Fiona. 'Have you got one too?'

She nodded, and instinctively her hand went to her chest, where another necklace must have sat beneath her coat.

'Are they to ward off evil spirits?' He laughed, a mocking, cruel laugh.

Fiona scowled, turned inward, and wouldn't look at them.

'They don't work, you know,' said Gus.

Storm shifted his weight and then bent his head to crop the sheep-bitten grass.

'Why don't you mind your own business?' said Ella.

'Fine,' he said. He smiled at her, but where before his smiles had felt like warmth from the sun, now he was all teeth and insincerity.

'Ask him about the kelpie,' said Fiona suddenly.

'What?' Ella looked at her sister, and all the things she'd forgotten rushed back into her head. The conversation she'd had with Gus about it, the glimpse she'd had of the faerie realm.

'What's a kelpie?' said Gus.

'You know what a kelpie is,' said Ella. 'You were the one who told me about it. The lake monster. The water horse. It's all true. It's followed our nan here from Scotland.'

'I don't know what you're talking about,' he said.

'You're a real pain, you know that?' said Ella. 'Let's just go home.'

'Hey, come on!' he said. 'Don't be like that!'

Ella ignored him and turned Magpie's head for home.

'Ella, Ella, Ella,' he sang.

Ella scowled. 'What?'

Gus's face fell. 'Ella, Ella, Ella,' he said again.

'Shut up.' She felt the talisman bumping against her collarbones as she urged Magpie into a slow jog. Then she noticed a black-tipped white feather caught in Magpie's mane. No, not caught, plaited in there. She

183

sniffed. Fiona must have put it there when she wasn't looking.

'Hey!' shouted Gus.

Ella stopped and turned around to look at him. His face had taken on dark clouds.

'Don't walk away from *me*,' he said, and for the first time Ella's trust in him fell away. Something was wrong. Magpie let out a piercing whinny, and Storm responded, suddenly agitated.

There was a loud humming in Ella's ears, and she pressed her hands to them, screwing up her face. The landscape undulated and the light turned a soft green, like sunlight falling through water. The rowan by the church gate waved like waterweeds in the soft breeze.

'No!' she shouted, and the vision dissolved. She was back by the church, with Gus and Fiona looking up at her. Magpie's flight response was kicking in; Ella felt energy surge through her, and she just managed to pull her left rein to her hip so Magpie's bolt turned into a tight circle and she was contained. For now.

'It's okay,' said Gus. 'You're not ready for that, I can tell. Maybe I'll show you in person soon, Ella, Ella.' The sound of his voice from his lips became the notes of the skylark building its tower of song up into the sky.

Ella touched the charm around her neck and the feeling dissipated.

'I'll race you home!' Gus called. He loosened Storm's reins but the bay horse stayed where he was, pawing the ground. 'Come on, ya useless beastie!' he shouted.

'We're not allowed to race the horses home,' Fiona said. 'We have to walk.'

'We'll see about that!' Gus said, and kicked Storm hard in the sides.

'Hey!' shouted Ella. 'Stop that!'

But Storm didn't gallop away. Instead he threw his head up and shook it, jangling the bit. He gave a squeal and pig-jumped, all four feet leaving the ground at once, straight up into the air. Gus kept his seat but yanked on the reins, wrenching Storm's mouth, and kicked him again. Then Storm, finally living up to his name, put his head down and bucked.

Gus flew into the air and landed *slub-slab* in a patch of mud.

16

Swither: to be uncertain as to
which course of action to choose

'Are you okay?' called Ella. She wanted to laugh, but she
thought she'd better check he was unhurt before she did.
Gus had landed on his front, arms and legs splayed, but
he'd managed to keep his face out of the mud. He pulled
himself up on his hands and knees, and crouched there,
taking deep breaths. Maybe he'd been winded. Storm
was pulling indignantly at some grass he'd found by a
gravestone.

Fiona came trotting over on Peedie, dismounted and
picked up Storm's reins before he could trip on them.
The two girls stared at Gus, waiting for him to respond.

The boy crawled out of the boggy patch and turned over to sit on the ground. His face was pink, and wet with tears. Whether they were tears of fury or pain, it was hard to tell.

Ella dismounted and went over to him. 'Can you stand up?' she asked.

She expected him to shout at her, to shout at Storm, but instead he wore a cloud of melancholy, and pity stirred inside her.

'I'm all right,' he said. 'But I can't see. Can you wipe my tears for me? My hands are all clarty.' He held them up to show her: muddy.

'Wipe them with what?' said Ella. 'Do you have a tissue?' She dug in her pocket but her finger touched something prickly. She pulled out the dried rowan sprig.

Gus threw up an arm. 'Not that!' he said. 'Put it away and use your hands to wipe them.' The tears continued to spill out of his eyes like a leaky tap; it was unnatural.

Ella shrugged and put the twig back in her pocket. 'Do you have a tissue, Fi?'

But Fiona was staring at Gus. Her body had begun to tremble. 'Don't do it,' she said, but her small voice was barely above a whisper.

'What?' said Ella, in case she had heard her wrong.

Fiona stared at her with a face that had never been so

determined. 'Don't do it!' she said again, almost shouting this time. 'Ellie, don't wipe his tears. Remember what Grizzly said about Aonghas Donn, about the kelpie. If you wipe his tears you'll be his! He's the kelpie, Ellie.' She was backing away from them now, one hand on Peedie's neck, moving towards the saddle.

Ella rolled her eyes and looked back at Gus.

Gus. *Aonghas.*

His wretched look of melancholy, devised to attract sympathy, was gone, replaced by what could only be described as malevolence. He jumped to his feet and wiped his hands on his pants. Then he rubbed his worn sleeve over his face, leaving streaks of dirt.

'You *stupid girl*,' he sneered. His eyes were no longer leaking. 'What are you talking about? Kelpie? I don't even know what that is. You're talking nonsense.'

'He's beglamoured you, Ellie,' said Fiona. 'That's why you can't see it. But I knew it as soon as I saw him.'

All those days of feeling like she was forgetting something — even now the image of the black horse on the shore of the lake was dim and misty, like an ill-remembered dream, making her doubt herself and what she had seen. It was all making sense now. And it had taken Fiona, and her funny homemade charms, to break the spell.

'Take off your helmet,' said Fiona.

He looked from one to the other of them, but didn't move.

'Yes,' said Ella. 'Take it off. This ride is over for you. You can walk home.'

'Fine,' he said, and unclipped the chin strap. He still wore his woollen hat underneath. He threw the helmet on the ground in front of Ella. She picked it up and handed it to Fiona, standing fortified by Peedie, who looked like he'd gone to sleep.

'Just one more thing,' said Ella, and she darted forward and snatched his hat from his head. Thick black hair sprang from beneath it.

'Look!' said Fiona.

Ella looked. And she saw. The weeds in his hair. How had she been so stupid? Glossy strands of waterweed glinted in the sunlight.

He touched them carelessly. 'It's nothing,' he said.

'We know what you are,' said Ella. 'You need to leave us alone!'

Gus put his head back and laughed. It was the laugh of an old man — ancient — who had fought many wars, and won them too. But his face remained young. Beautiful even. He was younger than the man Grizzly had fallen in love with — he was no more than thirteen

189

or fourteen — but there was no doubt it was the same person.

'You foolish girls. Don't you see? You need me. I can protect you. Protect you from all those men and boys in your life who want to do you harm. That boy, Josh. I couldn't believe it when you went out looking for him, wanted me to *help* you even! When it was *you* who wanted him gone.'

'Stop it,' said Ella. 'It's not true.' But she knew it was true. She'd known all along.

Gus went on. 'Those good-for-nothing men of Griselda's and her daughter's. They both wished them away, and I helped them with that wish.'

'No!' said Ella. 'They would never have done that. What do you mean?'

'They used to stand on the shore of that loch, arguing. I heard them. I couldn't come ashore back then, not with all that blasted rowan around, but I made sure that Griselda's husband never came home. Your mother told her husband that he should stay away for good if he liked the loch better than home. Well, I took care of that, too. I gave him the ride of his life.'

Ella went to her sister, and the two girls put their arms around each other. Ella had the urge to put her hands over Fiona's ears so she wouldn't have to listen.

'And as for that pony of yours. Ungrateful wretch. I gave her to you and she repays me by biting me. If she wasn't my own kin I'd drown her in the loch just like I drowned the rest of them. But don't cry,' he said. 'I did it all for you, don't you see? For Griselda, the love of my life. To keep you all safe.'

'She doesn't want you!' said Fiona. 'You're a monster!'

'I told you, *I'm not a monster!*' With those words, his voice changed, low and gurgling, like bubbling mud. His face took on a sallow look, yellow and green. How had Ella ever seen anything in him? 'If she won't come back to me, then I'll take the things that matter from her until she does. You have been warned.'

He lunged forward and grabbed his hat back, just as Magpie stretched out her neck and sank her teeth into his arm.

Gus yelled and gripped his wrist, pushing his sleeve back. But when he pulled his hand away, there was no mark. He laughed.

'I don't need you — either of you — or your stupid horses.' He shook his hair out of his eyes and replaced the hat on his head, as casual as you like. 'You think you're protected by those ridiculous things you've got around your necks? Those *charms*? You think your family is safe? You'll never be safe. You'll never be rid of me. You'll see.'

He turned and with wide strides leapt away from them, running until he disappeared over the brow of the hill. They were alone with just the sound of distant thunder, or beating hooves.

'WE SHOULD GET HOME,' Ella said eventually. 'We should tell Grizzly what happened.' They stood, dumbstruck, in the shadow of the church, holding on to their ponies as well as Storm.

Magpie nudged Ella in the shoulder, and Ella laid her face on her soft muzzle. 'I trust you completely,' she said in answer to her unasked question. 'Don't I, girl? You wouldn't bite me.'

Magpie blew warm air through her nose instead.

Ella thought back to the way Magpie had behaved over the last few days. Yes, she had been agitated and skittish, aggressive even. But it had always been when Gus was around. She was sure now that Gus had been the one to tell Dominic to ride her. He'd known how she would behave, and he had plotted to get rid of her. Magpie wasn't a danger to other riders — only Gus. And only because she was trying to protect them. Just as he'd said, horses had a much more acute sense of danger, seeing the dark shadows, invisible to humans, inside the darkest of corners.

Ella felt relief then, and closed her eyes, not quite believing what had happened to them, the crushing danger they had avoided. Did Magpie know about the kelpie? That she was its offspring?

A crash came from inside the church. The girls looked at each other in alarm.

'We should go now,' said Fiona, worry crowding her voice.

A ragged shadow rose from the hole in the church's roof, a fluting note followed by a squawk.

Ella blinked into the sunlight. 'Just a magpie. Come on, let's go home.'

They mounted the ponies, and Ella took Storm's reins from Fiona to lead him. They began the sedate walk home.

As they descended, they spotted the trekkers on the bridle path that skirted around the hill below them, but instead of a neat line of horses, plodding quietly, the line was a chaotic scribble. A ripple seemed to pass through the horses. They were agitated, watching something.

And there it was. The black horse. The kelpie.

It looked huge, even from so far away. Ella watched from above as the scene played out like a silent film. Magpie tensed beneath her.

'What should we do?' asked Fiona.

'Just wait, Fi,' said Ella. 'It's not safe.'

'It's like a dream horse,' said Fiona. 'I see it in my dreams. I think it's always been there, waiting to come out.'

Ella's mind stirred, her unconscious waking up long enough to give her a glimpse of something deep inside before it sank back into the darkness.

'Me too,' she said. 'I think it's always been with us, as long as we've been alive.'

DOWN BELOW, HANA was at the front of the pack, now a cluster. Morag was behind, standing in her stirrups. There it was. The black horse. It was huge — eighteen hands high at least, towering over them and gazing at them with its nose in the air.

'What a beauty,' one of the riders had said, but their admiration had turned to discomfort when the horses started to bunch together.

'Steady,' Morag called as the horse's head swung this way and that, taking them all in almost greedily. Gazing at them as though it was the leader of the herd. Morag tried to ease Duke forward, past the rider in front of her, but the track was narrow and there was a steep drop on one side. She was cragfast, with no room to turn around and no way to go forward while the black stallion was in front of them.

'What should we do?' called Hana. Morag heard the waver in her voice. She was scared. Brilliant, brave Hana was scared.

'Hold fast,' called Morag down to the front. 'He's a big fella, isn't he?'

The horses were scared now too. They started to back away from the animal, jamming their tails into each other's faces. One of the girls let out a stifled scream of surprise. The horses were quivering — was it fear, or excitement?

Suddenly the stallion reared and let out a deep rumble. The horses jostled each other like sheep being trucked to the abattoir. The sides of the track began to crumble, and lumps of clay and dirt rattled down the hill. The black horse towered over them, seemed to hang in the air before crashing down, barely missing Hana, who ducked low over her horse's shoulder. Then the stallion was leaping as though winged, down the hill.

Morag let out the breath she'd been holding, but too soon: the next moment there was a scream, and Olive, the albino mare, was hurtling head first down the near-vertical slope. The woman riding her managed to hold on by leaning right back in the saddle, but it was impossible.

'Hold your reins tight!' shouted Morag to the other riders. 'Don't let them have their heads!'

The woman tumbled off Olive and lay still as the mare leapt ahead, down, down towards the shore of the lake, where the black horse was waiting for her.

'Hana!' shouted Morag. 'Can you reach her?'

The fallen rider was sitting up now. She turned and raised a hand. 'I'm okay,' she called, though her voice was breathy, as if she'd had the wind knocked out of her. She turned onto her hands and knees and began climbing back up the slope.

The black horse stood at the bottom of the hill with Olive, her reins broken and trailing on the ground. The two stood nose to nose, though Olive had to reach her head up to meet him. Morag couldn't help but gasp. They made a beautiful pair — the treacle black and the milky white. She shook the thought away.

Now that the group was safely on the other side of the track, Morag told Hana to take the others back, slowly. The horses were restless; some of them stooped to try to pull on the tussocky grass; others were still tossing their heads, bits jangling. It felt chaotic, the last thing she wanted.

'Put Olive's rider on Rocky,' Morag said. 'You'll have to walk beside her. I don't want anything else spooking them today.'

'What will you do?' asked Hana as she dismounted.

Morag's face was determined. 'I'm going to get Olive. I don't like her chances with that stallion.'

'Be careful,' said Hana. 'It's wild. I've never seen it before. Do you know who it belongs to?'

Morag shook her head. 'I'll ask around once we're back in the house, but now I just need to get my mare back.'

She turned Duke for the more sedate track down towards the lake, and urged him into a canter. She was going to rescue that horse at any cost.

ONCE THE KELPIE had disappeared down the hill, and Olive with it, Ella knew she and Fiona needed to make a move. She had seen Hana gather the riders together and start leading them back through the gate the way they had come. They would meet up at the bottom of the paddock.

Hana was flushed, not her usual composed self. She was trying to direct everyone from the ground, and was leading the woman who had fallen from Olive and now sagged, looking green, in Rocky's saddle.

'Oh thank goodness,' she said when she saw the girls. 'And a spare horse! What happened to Storm's rider? Actually never mind, just give him here.' Ella handed over the reins, and Hana mounted. 'Your mum's gone after that huge stallion. You won't believe what happened! I'm glad you're here — I need your help getting everyone back safely. The horses are spooked and I'm terrified of what they might do next. If I go in front, you can take the rear. And look after Fiona too.'

'I'm fine,' said Fiona indignantly. 'Peedie will look after me.'

'I have to go with Mum,' said Ella.

'No,' said Hana. 'She'll be okay. You need to come with me. Haere mai.'

Ella swithered: Hana needed her to help get the riders back to the yard, but her mother needed her more — she just didn't know it yet. There was a risk of getting in trouble — or she might just save her mother's life. It was no longer a difficult decision.

'Please. Magpie will know what to do.'

'How can Magpie . . . no. That's not going to happen. Ella. *Ella*—'

But Ella had turned Magpie's head back the way Morag had gone.

'I'm sorry!' she called.

'Ella!' Hana cried in frustration, but it was too late. Ella urged Magpie into a canter, and Magpie needed no encouragement — she flew through the air and made the wind sing in their ears.

17

Down, down, towards the lake they flew, down the twisty track, through the stand of wilding pines — Magpie knew exactly how close she could get to them without knocking Ella off. She cleared the low fallen logs on the shortcut as if they were made of air, and then they emerged into the bright afternoon, onto the bridle path by the lake. Magpie was huffing, her neck wet with sweat, when Ella pulled her up.

From a distance she watched her mother and Duke approach the mare and the stallion, picking their way slowly over the rocky part of the shoreline near the mouth of the river. Ella hesitated for a moment, then urged Magpie left along the track that led above the shore — she could move faster that way and keep her approach concealed from sight, if not from hearing.

When she drew level with them, Morag was off Duke and was stepping gingerly over the stones towards the horses. The stallion was circling Olive in much the same way it had circled the horses in the paddock in Ella's dream. It was trotting, bringing its knees high, its tail proud and flowing behind it, making a ring, and then turning and trotting in the opposite direction. Olive trembled in the middle. She was under its spell and it was clear that she was frightened out of her wits. The stallion's hooves rang hollow on the stones and sand, kicking up dust. High above, a lone magpie circled, not daring to swoop.

Ella had to get Morag away from there. She was in danger. An image came into her head of that day on the shore when she had been inexplicably drawn to the horse, then again of the terrible teeth that grew from its jaws, sharp and menacing, grabbing the birds and tearing them apart.

'Mum!' she called out. Morag had been creeping closer and closer. She looked like she was about to make a run for it, to grab Olive's broken reins and try to lead her away to where dependable old Duke stood nearby.

Morag's head snapped around. The look on her face was startled, then determined. She held her hand up and mouthed *Go, get back*. Behind her, the stallion had stopped trotting and was staring intently at Morag. Suddenly, it started towards her at a fast walk. Morag turned back, and her arms dropped by her side. Ella watched with dread as the horse walked right up to her mother and breathed on her face. Why wasn't Morag moving away? Instead, she put up a hand and touched the horse's nose. A ripple went through its coat, the black glimmering with green and silver.

Ella realised with horror what was about to happen. She remembered how it had felt, how being near the horse had filled her body with light and warmth, and how irresistible it was.

Morag started to move slowly towards the stallion's neck, trailing her hand as she went. It was only a matter of seconds before she'd be on its back, pulled by an unseen force that would defy gravity.

Magpie reacted before Ella did. She took off at a gallop towards woman and horse, leaping off the track and onto the shore. The black horse raised its head and let out a deep rumbling whinny, a challenge. Magpie slowed for a second, then plunged on, just in time. The horse backed away a few steps, and Morag turned around to look, blinking, as Ella and her pony approached. They pulled up beside her. Ella's heart was pounding but she let Magpie move to stand between her mother and the stallion.

'What the hell . . . ?' said Morag, and Ella put out a hand.

'Trust me, Mum, please. You have to get out of here. Back away. *Now!*'

Morag opened her mouth as if to speak, but closed it again, and for once she listened to her daughter. She was pale and wide-eyed. Ella had never seen her look so bewildered; Morag always knew what to do in every situation. Now she looked confused and shocked. But she nodded and started to back away, as if deep down she knew what was going on and that somehow Ella and Magpie knew best.

The stallion reared and lashed out with its hooves, narrowly missing Magpie's head. But the little horse stood her ground, trembling. For long seconds, the two horses stood eyeballing each other, until a plaintive whinny echoed out across the shore of the lake. Olive. She still stood rooted to the ground. The sound snapped the tension between the horses. The stallion tossed its head and took two steps back, bringing its hooves to the ground with a thud. Then it wheeled on its back legs and took off at a fast trot, its neck arched. It resumed its circle around Olive once, twice, then it kicked up sand and launched itself towards the lake, away from Ella and Magpie and Morag and Duke. Olive followed without hesitation, but her eyes were wild and her neck was dark with sweat. Her broken reins swung dangerously around her. Ella and Morag braced for the moment she would step on them, fall and break her neck. But it didn't come.

The stallion entered the lake at a slow canter, splashing in the shallows, sending up a fan of droplets. It loped in slow strides out across the water as if it was a mere puddle, even though the colour of the lake changed to a deep blue as the lakebed fell away into the depths. On it went, gliding across the surface.

'What the hell?' said Morag again.

Olive entered the lake not far behind, head high, following. For a moment she too drummed into the shallows, but within moments the water reached her knees and slowed her down. She didn't stop though; she continued on through the water.

'No,' said Morag. She put her foot in the stirrup and swung onto Duke's back, then urged him towards the lake, where Olive was struggling now, on, on towards the black stallion, which had stopped and was turned towards her, standing solid on the water as if it was made of thick ice. It let out a long, lingering nicker. Olive responded, but it was laboured. The water reached her neck, then her head. She swam now, only the top of her head showing, nostrils high, and then she was gone.

The stallion reared one last time, leapt high in the air, plunged, and was also gone, leaving only a radiating circle of ripples.

Morag had reached the water's edge, where she pulled off her jacket and dropped it on the sand before urging Duke in, clattering and splashing madly. Duke resisted, so she threw herself off and began wading through the water, crying 'Olive!' Then she was swimming while Ella watched with tears wetting her cheeks. Morag dived and kept swimming, out into the lake, stopping and turning circles, trying to see into the water, but it was useless. Olive was gone. The lake, and the kelpie, had taken her.

18

Glamourie: an enchantment

'It was chaos!' Hana was saying. 'We never should have taken the horses out after being cooped up for so long. We should have given them a day in the paddock to work out their energy.'

Morag was subdued, listening and nodding, not her usual fiery self. 'Tell me again what happened. Slowly this time.'

Hana took a deep slow breath, then began again. 'We got past the steep part of the track okay, but when we got to the paddock — you know, the one we canter in — we heard this noise, this unbelievably eerie sound.

Did you hear it too? It was like the whinny of that black horse but it was everywhere. It rumbled all around us. I could feel it through my bones.' She glanced at one of the riders, who nodded.

'Well, the horses went crazy. They started shying and carrying on — young Matilda fell off, but she was okay — and then they did what we've tried so hard to prevent. They bolted. Every single one of them. Except Peedie. Thank goodness. Fiona's fine, she's gone inside the house with Griselda.' Hana's voice was shaking. 'When the horses got to the gate, they jumped it. There was screaming — Morag, it was horrible. And a couple more riders fell off. I managed to calm Storm enough — well, you know him, nothing much fazes him — and I picked them up, then tried to get back here as quietly but quickly as I could.'

The horses had headed straight for home and had calmed down as soon as they entered the yard. The riders had tethered and untacked their horses, then moved to the barn where they were now drinking tea. They were shaken but not angry, Hana said. They understood that something extraordinary had happened. Morag looked relieved to hear this. The last thing she needed was another scandal — it could finish the trekking business off.

Morag was shivering with the cold in her wet clothes. She'd at least had the foresight to remove her jacket before entering the water, but it was now soaked through from the inside. Ella watched as her mother, wrapped in a dirty straw-coloured blanket she must have found in the barn, set her shoulders straight and made her way over to talk to the riders.

She was amazed at her mother's strength, and with a wash of shame realised she'd never really thought about it before. Morag just *was*. She was her mother. Businesslike, brusque, but also soft and dependable. She was carrying the weight of their whole family on her shoulders. The stables, raising two children without their father, her mother now sick and with probably not long to live . . .

Earlier, at the lake, Morag had waded out and Ella had met her at the water's edge, handing her the jacket she'd picked up off the stones. Her mother was pale, with blue lips, and her teeth chattered.

'I lost her,' Morag said in a small voice. She crouched down and gave a loud groan, knocking with her knuckles on the riding helmet she still wore. When she stood up again, her eyes were red and moist. 'Gah. I couldn't save her, Ellie. It's that keld. It must have acted like a whirl-pool and sucked her under. But how? There's no sign of her.' As if to confirm it, she turned and looked back out over the lake. It was still and quiet, with only the sound of the water's edge gently frilling the stones. A slow, thin mist was rolling across from the other side of the lake, and the sky had become grey and sulky.

Neither of them mentioned it, but the fact hung in the air between them. This was the same spot Ella's father had gone missing. The river mouth was his favourite fishing spot, for the salmon and trout that swam up and down the river and into the lake.

Ella moved forward and her mother embraced her. They held each other for a long time while Morag's wet clothes seethed with damp. Beside them, Magpie hung her head.

They didn't speak much on the way back. There was a cloud of unspoken fear hanging over them. Namely, the kelpie. Because that is what it was. It had cantered across the surface of the water as if on earth, and it had dived under, and it would rise again. What did it want?

'Mum, that horse, what we saw—' Ella ventured, just once.

Her mother closed her down. 'Let's not talk about that, Ellie. Nobody will believe it, and I'm not sure I believe it myself. The less we say the better. We need to get home.'

BACK AT THE stables, as Ella stood watching Morag through the open doors of the barn, Hana came up beside her and said, 'Oi, hōhā. I'm not happy with you. We might have prevented all that if you'd been there.'

Ella looked at her, defiant. She wasn't going to feel guilty on top of everything they'd been through. She knew she'd made the right choice. Who knows what might have happened to Morag if she hadn't gone with her? 'You don't really think that, do you?' she said. 'What could I have done?'

'You could have brought up the rear of the group while I led. Created some order. I don't know. What happened to Olive? Did you find her? I'm guessing not.'

'Oh, we found her all right,' said Ella quietly. She told Hana about Olive following the stallion into the water, but she left out the part where it walked on water. How could she explain that? That her family had brought a lake monster here to this beautiful place where Hana's ancestors had lived for hundreds of years? She felt a creeping sensation that she recognised as shame.

'Oh, no. No,' cried Hana. She hurried towards the barn, just as Morag was coming out, drying herself, still looking deathly cold, and threw her arms around her. Morag looked surprised and a bit stiff before she accepted the hug. When they pulled apart, she averted her eyes.

'I'm so sorry about Olive,' said Hana.

'Yes, well.' Morag started walking away towards the house. 'I'm sorry I can't help you anymore. I need to have a shower and get warmed up. Can you see the horses all get put away? Can you help her, Ella?' She didn't wait for an answer. But when she reached the path to the house, she turned and called back. 'I'm sorry about today, Hana. And thank you. I don't know what we'd do without you. Take tomorrow off. I've got to run some pony rides at the spring fair, not that I want to. But it's to raise money for Josh Underhill's family and I've made a promise.'

Hana raised a hand in answer, then turned to Ella.

'Right, you. It's been a hard day. Let's get these horses sorted and say haere rā to this lot.'

Magpie was reluctant to leave when Ella turned her out. She stood leaning her head against Ella's arm while having her forelock stroked. Ella wondered how much the pony understood about what had happened. She could hardly make sense of it herself.

How on earth could she get her head around the fact that the kelpie was also Gus?

Now that they had unmasked him, she felt sure that the horse was his true form on land, the human form a trick: glamourie. She remembered his words: *You think your family is safe? You'll never be safe. You'll never be rid of me.* Ella had heard about people who became obsessed with another person, a love interest, and followed them, watched them, harmed them, all in the name of what they mistook for love. There was a name for them.

Stalker.

Aonghas Donn had stalked Grizzly. He had followed her here and now he was stalking them all, trying to trick Ella into friendship the way he'd tricked Grizzly into love. But Fiona had seen through him. Her funny little charms had held him at bay long enough for Ella to see the truth. Who knows what would have happened to her otherwise?

RITA WAS IN the kitchen, wiping down the bench, when Ella came in. Warm smells came from a pot on the stove, with notes of fresh bread from the oven. Rita paused to wipe her pink face with the back of her hand and smiled.

'Soup's on, bread's in the oven. I just had a feeling you'd need it tonight,' she said, 'and I was right. The last thing your mum needs to do right now is have to cook dinner on top of everything else. You can save Hana's mum's casserole for tomorrow.'

Her kindness melted something inside Ella, and her eyes filled with tears.

'Oh, hey,' said Rita, coming out from behind the bench. 'Oh, you poor love. It's all a bit much for you, isn't it?' She gathered Ella into a hug. She smelled of disinfectant and woodsmoke. She must've lit the fire as well.

Ella pulled away. 'Why are you so nice to us?'

Rita looked shocked. She shook her head and her frizzy red hair bobbed. 'What do you mean, pet?'

'Everyone else in town avoids us. They think we're witches. Weirdos. They think that we had something to do with Dad and Grandad going missing. I see them when we go shopping. They look away, but they stare at us when they think we can't see them.' She pictured them as birds, with blade wings and sharp claws, with necks that could turn unnaturally far to watch you as you went by. 'We don't like going into town. The kids at school won't talk to me. Their parents tell them to stay away, I know they do. So why don't you?'

'You've never said this to me before. Oh, love, I didn't know things were so hard for you. I didn't know that about the school. Why have you never told me?'

Ella just shrugged. She'd always liked Rita, she supposed, but Rita was from town, so she had never got too close.

'They don't know anything, those people. They don't

213

know you like I do. I care about you all. Yes, it's my job, but I see how hard your mum works. I know what you've all gone through. It's been such a privilege, getting to know you all. Your gran's a crack-up. It's an honour to care for her. I always admired what she did, how she stopped that dairy farm. She's a brave, special lady, and I'll miss her . . .' She trailed off.

'No,' said Ella. 'Don't. She's just sick, that's all. She'll hang on.'

Rita took a big breath in through her nose and stood up straighter. She placed her hands on Ella's shoulders and squeezed. 'Just talk to her,' she said. 'I'll give you a tray to take to her. And talk to your mum. You need each other right now.'

19

Ella pushed open the door to Grizzly's room. The curtains were closed, but a small lamp created a soft kernel of light over a bedside table filled with pill bottles, a jug of water, a clock and a stack of crossword books. Grizzly's grimoire was perched on top.

The room was the cleanest in the house, thanks to Rita, and it carried her disinfectant smell. Grizzly lay back on brightly coloured pillows, her white hair spread around her. Fiona was sitting with her, holding her hand. Grizzly looked up, and though she was diminished, and pale, her black eyes shone in the lamplight. Ella got the feeling she had interrupted something, that they had been talking and had stopped when she came in. She felt a stab of jealousy.

'Thank you, my lovely,' said Grizzly. Her voice was weak. 'Just put it on the dresser there — I can see the steam coming off it.'

Ella did as she was told.

'Sit down, lass.' She patted the mattress on the opposite side to where Fiona sat. Her other hand was still gripped by Fiona's small pale one.

Ella felt shy suddenly. She sat.

'Fiona here's been telling me about your adventures.'

Ella nodded. What else could she say?

'So that Aonghas Donn is back. And he tried to come for my babies. If he hurts you, I'll kill him, so help me.'

'Grizzly!' Ella was shocked.

'Ach, he's no' a boy if that's what you're worried about. I wouldn't kill a boy. But a nasty loch monster, now that's another story. A cursed water sprite.'

'There's more,' said Ella. 'The horse came. The horse came and it took Olive.'

Fiona gasped. Of course she hadn't heard about it; she'd been back in the house by the time Morag and Ella had returned. Her face grew pink and two tears spilled down her cheeks.

'What's this?' Morag stood in the doorway in her fluffy dressing gown, drying her hair with a towel.

'The kelpie took Olive, Mum,' wailed Fiona.

'No, no, love,' said Morag, dropping the towel and coming into the room. She reached out to touch Fiona's shoulder. 'Olive was just confused. She got herself in trouble and she sank — I couldn't save her. I did try, I promise.'

'Ach,' said Grizzly, frowning. 'Don't lie to the bairn, woman. She's not stupid, you know. She knows what's what. You can't tell me that blasted black horse didn't have something to do with it. Ach, away wi' ye.' She shook her head and set her mouth as though she'd tasted something disgusting.

'I knew it!' said Fiona.

'Is there anything else you're not telling us?' said Grizzly.

Ella stayed silent and looked at Morag, who refused to meet her eyes and busied herself picking the towel up from the floor and folding it. The silence was thick and dank.

Finally, Ella couldn't hold it in.

'It galloped on the water! It lured Olive in, and she couldn't keep up with it, and she was pulled under. Right in the calm patch of water, near the river mouth. Then it dived under too.'

Morag made a scoffing noise. 'Don't talk nonsense, Ella. It was just a trick of the light. It must have been on a sandbar of some kind underwater. It's not Jesus, you know! It's only a horse.'

'The keld, is it?' said Grizzly, ignoring her daughter. 'I always knew that place was thin.'

'Thin?' asked Fiona.

'You remember me saying earlier? A place where our world butts up against the other place, the one where kelpies dwell. He had to have come up from somewhere. I knew that mare must have been under his spell.'

'Well, I think you're right about one thing,' said Morag. 'That stallion is most likely Magpie's sire, given how we never did find out how she got with foal. But it was years ago. Why has it only shown up again now?'

'That thing has been waiting patiently for a long time. But also time moves differently for the likes of Aonghas Donn. A year, a day, a minute — it's all the same. Something's brought him back. He saw an opportunity with that boy.'

Ella remembered her wish that night — how she'd wished for a friend on the very day she'd cursed Josh. That was when he'd shown up again. She'd invited the devil into their lives.

'He took my Bobby,' Grizzly went on. 'Of course he did. And I'll not be surprised if he took your Will too. Leaving these poor wee girls without a father. We've been cursed, our whole family, since I first laid eyes on him.'

'Stop!' said Morag. 'You're not making any sense, Mum. Dad and Will drowned by accident. Just horrible accidents.'

'Then why did they never find Will? Hm? Surely you have asked yourself that?'

'Of course I've asked myself that. Don't you think I've asked it every night when I wake up and can't get back to sleep? Around and around it goes in my head. Every night when I get into a cold bed and every day when I have to do everything around here by myself. How could you even ask me that?' She covered her face with both hands.

Ella saw a picture in her mind of that day, of her father waving cheerfully as he set off for his special fishing spot halfway around the lake. He was wearing a funny floppy hat, with a vest he kept all his flies and packets of mints in, and anything else he might need. He bopped Ella on the nose, said, 'See you tonight, kiddo,' and drove away. Fiona was crying inside the house, and Ella thought she would like to get away for some peace and quiet, too, and wished he had taken her with him.

After he disappeared, she had lain awake in the dark too. She had got up and stood outside her mother's door, wanting to go inside and climb into bed with her, like she had when Dad was there, before Fiona was born, shimmying down under the covers between them. But the stillness and coldness that always radiated from under her mother's door made her turn back to bed. She had never even considered that her mother was also awake, going over and over what could have happened to him and why her husband hadn't been found. That she got up every morning and carried on caring for them, changing their lives to adapt to his absence. How her hair had turned grey so fast, and her cheeks took on a hollowed look, where before they had been plump and squeezable, so soft when she cuddled them.

'He's going to come back one day,' said Ella quietly. 'We would know if he was dead. We would know.'

'Ella, so help me, I wish you were right,' said Morag. 'I wish it was just that he had abandoned us. That it all became too much for him and he slipped away into the night. But I knew him. I *knew* him. And it's time for you to accept that your father isn't just gone, he's dead. Drowned in that great black bottomless lake.'

'The kelpie,' said Fiona.

'No, Fi, no.'

Ella looked at her mother, who was as sure that her husband had drowned as Ella was that he was still alive somewhere. And Grizzly and Fiona were just as sure that he'd been taken by the kelpie. Which of them was right? Either way, the conviction that her father would come home again was slipping away. It was time for her to be brave, to accept reality. She felt the last little piece of him lift away from her then, and drift up into the warm, sterile-smelling room. A trickle of sadness, like cold water, replaced it.

'All right, love, all right,' Grizzly was saying. 'I don't like it any more than you do. I thought we just had bad luck. But now I know it wasn't luck. It was a curse. And we have to find some way to break it.'

Morag ran a hand through her hair. 'Mum, you're scaring the children.'

'Good! They should be scared. I'm not long for this world and we need to break this thing before I go. We're running out of time.'

'Don't say that, Grizzly,' pleaded Ella. 'You're going to get better.' A plan was formulating in her head. If they could only get rid of the kelpie, break the curse, then somehow Grizzly would regain her strength.

'No, my lovely,' said Grizzly. She sighed. She looked so tired — more tired than Ella had ever seen her.

Fiona leaned forward until her head lay on Grizzly's lap. Grizzly put out a hand and stroked her hair.

'Have you told them yet?' Grizzly asked.

Morag had been about to speak, but she closed her mouth, looking ashamed. She shook her head.

'Told us what?' said Ella, but she didn't want to know.

'That I can see the end now. I'm ready. I'm so tired, girls. So, so tired. And I want you to know that I love you, and I would do anything for you. Anything. But I want to go home now. I want to go home. But before I go, we have to stop the kelpie or he will haunt you the rest of your lives.'

She closed her eyes and took a deep breath. Ella could hear it wheezing in her chest. Then she went still. Ella stared at her, waiting for her to open her eyes again.

'Grizzly!' she shouted, panicked. She might have let go of her father, but she wasn't going to let her grand-mother go too.

'Ow, girl, I'm not dead yet! I was just resting my eyes.'

'Sorry,' said Ella.

'Look,' said Morag, folding her arms. 'I don't know about this kelpie business but we do have to catch that horse.'

'Can we trap it?' said Ella. 'Magpie's not afraid of it. She can help.'

'But what do we do with it once we've trapped it?' said Morag. 'We can't just send it off to the knacker's yard.'

'What's that?' said Fiona.

'It's where they make dog food,' said Ella.

Fiona widened her eyes. 'No! You can't kill it!'

Grizzly squeezed her hand. 'It's not a horse, remember? It's me he wants. He's followed me here. Ach, this country. We've ruined it in so many ways. Cleared all that forest, destroyed all those native birds and plants just so we can make it look like home. Putting dairy farms where they have no business, destroying the land and the beautiful waterways. And yes, I've not helped, planting my rowan. But now I've also brought this monster. It doesn't belong here, and though I'm not sure we belong here either, I love this country like it was my own and would do anything to save it.'

There was silence then, and Ella became aware of the ticking of the clock on Grizzly's dressing table.

Grizzly spoke again. 'I'll think about it and come up with a plan. There must be something we can do. Kelpies don't like iron, or metal of any kind. But especially iron.'

'That's right,' said Ella, remembering now. 'Gus hated the bits on the horses. And using a saddle. He was really awkward with the stirrups. I don't think I ever saw him touch them directly. And he wouldn't go into the church.'

'The iron gate,' said Grizzly, nodding.

'The gate was down though, on the ground. But he'd

still have to step over it. And the rowan. Might that have stopped him? He never came to the house. He wanted to meet you but he never tried to come inside.'

'Rowan was a deterrent, of course. I'm not sure it would have injured him, like iron would, but yes, I do think it's kept him away from us for a long time. The rowan at home in Scotland didn't save us; it must have been too far from the door. Though god knows my mother was superstitious enough to have all kinds of other charms nailed above it. They clearly didn't work.'

'Fiona's did,' said Ella, and she looked at her sister, who had been listening so quietly. 'I think I was beglamoured, Grizzly. I think the charms helped.'

Fiona just nodded, and Grizzly looked at her with pride. 'And did you find yourself forgetting things?' Grizzly said. 'Couldn't quite remember him sometimes, or didn't make the connection between that boy and my story? Aye, that's glamourie all right. He was doing that to you, ya poor wee thing.'

'Well, I can't sit around here doing nothing,' said Morag. 'Whatever the horse is, it's a menace. I'll ring around and see if we can get someone to help. Surely if it's a menace to us, it's a menace to everyone around here.'

'You think they'll listen to the likes of you?' said Grizzly, looking doubtful.

'They have to,' said Morag. 'Someone will want to keep it, surely. It's a valuable animal. It must belong to *someone*.' She spoke these last few words as if to herself as she slipped out the door.

Grizzly and the girls looked at one another.

'She still thinks it's just a horse,' said Fiona. 'Why can't she see?'

Grizzly sighed. 'There's so much magic flying around, I don't know what's what.'

'The kelpie nearly took her,' said Ella. 'Today, by the lake. She was going to jump on its back. Magpie saved her.'

'Ach, maybe there's still remnants of the spell attached to her.'

'It nearly took me, too, Grizzly. I tried to tell you, but . . .'

'You couldn't make the words? It was like a dream?'

Ella nodded. 'What can we do?' She felt exhausted suddenly. Everything felt hopeless.

'We'll sleep on it, love.'

'I'll talk to it,' Fiona said quietly, but she was drowned out by the sound of Morag in the next room. Her voice was raised, outraged. Then silent as she dialled another number. They listened intently, and heard her voice get louder once again.

'I'll do it myself!' she yelled at last. There was a clattering sound, as if she had thrown her phone down onto the kitchen bench in disgust.

'Mum?' Ella called.

Morag came into the bedroom. The exhaustion of the day had caught up with her. She was hollow-eyed and furious.

'We don't need them,' she said. 'None of them will help us. We'll have to find a way to trap it ourselves. We'll do it tomorrow.'

'Isn't it the spring fair tomorrow?' asked Grizzly. 'Didn't you make a promise?'

'Ugh,' said Morag. 'Why should I bother?'

'It's for Josh,' said Fiona.

Morag's look softened then. The hardness under the skin collapsed. She sighed. 'Right. Yes, for Josh. Remember to write on my grave when I'm gone, girls: "Here lies Morag. She did unto others as she would have others do unto her."'

'That's the spirit,' said Grizzly. 'Don't let the beggars grind you down. Now hand me that soup, will you, Ella? I think it must have cooled by now.'

20

That night, Ella was once again plagued by dreams that made no sense. In one dream, the door in her mind unlocked, like an ungiving, and the images Gus had planted in there took seed and grew. She was floating in space that was green and gold, and she sensed others near her, suspended, waiting. They were murky, indistinct shapes in the ether. Once again she felt the world rather than just seeing it, but her human senses couldn't understand the messages they were receiving. It reminded her of a lesson she'd had once at school, where the teacher explained that if we lived in a two-dimensional world, everything would be flat, like a drawing. If a three-dimensional person suddenly appeared, we would only perceive them as they intersected with our world — as footprints. Maybe it was like that — Ella could only perceive the kelpie's realm where it aligned with what she already knew: colours, shapes, taste, smell, sounds and touch. She was at once underwater and somewhere else, and her skin tingled with something like electricity. She didn't belong here, but she felt a pull, an intense curiosity. It was outside time and everything.

She woke sweaty, disoriented, to find Fiona standing over her.

'Did you have the dream too?' asked Ella.

Fiona nodded. 'I think Josh was there. And there were others. I think they were watching over us.'

'Don't be scared,' said Ella, though she didn't really know why. Fiona had every reason to be as terrified as she was. She was surprised when Fiona, who usually saw right through false brightness, said, 'Don't worry. I'm not scared,' and squeezed her wrist. She had the knowing look she sometimes got that made Ella feel young and small next to her.

All treks were cancelled for the day — Morag was reluctant to admit it, but she was spooked by what had happened and didn't want to risk another incident.

'I think we could all do with a bit of a rest, the horses included,' she said. 'I'll ask around at the fair today and see if anyone knows who owns the horse and how we can catch it.'

'You haven't listened to a word I've said, have you?' said Grizzly. She sat on the sofa, bundled in a blanket. Her skin had a yellow pallor. 'You'll not catch that creature, and it belongs to no one.'

Morag ignored her. 'I've promised to give pony rides at the fair, so I'll take Peedie down in the float. Do you girls want to come?'

Ella thought about seeing all the townspeople, about seeing Josh's mother again, the accusing look in her eyes. Ella's family might not have done anything to hurt Josh, but the creeping realisation that the kelpie might have taken him made her feel guilty somehow.

'No, I'm tired,' she said simply, truthfully.

'Can you mind Fiona then? I can't really look out for her while I'm busy with the pony. I can always come and get you if you change your mind. Grizzly could do with the company too, since it's Rita's day off.'

Ella nodded as she scooped the last of the porridge from her bowl.

'And when did you last have a shower?' her mother went on. 'Days ago, I'll bet. Call me straight away if you think Grizzly needs me, or call Rita. And you know the emergency number. If it's an emergency, call an ambulance.'

'What kind of emergency?' asked Ella.

'A medical emergency. You'll know. And listen. I've thought about this, and I'm not going to mention how we lost Olive, not today anyway. It's too hard to explain. I'll just say she's gone missing and ask about the black horse.'

ELLA SADDLED UP Magpie while Fiona pottered around in the barn, picking up straw and hay and stuffing them into a sack. They were going to stay nice and safe, away from the lake, away from the Ben, and Ella would practise her jumping in the arena. Resentment fizzed inside her then. The kelpie had taken away their feeling of freedom, of safety.

Fiona dragged the sack out of the barn, heading for the meadow behind the house, where the stone circle was, and where the wildflowers were starting to bloom.

'Just stay where I can see you,' Ella called, watching her go. Fiona was wearing her usual yellow coat, despite the warm breeze, with gumboots and striped leggings. She looked like a character from a story book.

Ella led Magpie to the arena, where a few jumps were set up in the centre — a couple of cavalletti, a cross rail and two verticals. Hana had been giving her lessons here on quiet days, and she hadn't practised all holidays. From a distance, she saw Fiona drop her sack in the circle and start to pick flowers — cornflowers and poppies, and others she couldn't identify. A couple of magpies alighted on the stones and kept watch. Satisfied her sister wasn't going anywhere, Ella mounted to begin her warm-up.

She was impressed by how far Magpie had come. She could jump a little over a metre now, the same as the wooden and wire fences that circled the paddocks, and higher than the old drystone walls scattered around the landscape. But after twenty minutes in the arena Magpie grew impatient with jumping and started bucking into her canters, tossing her head after each successful attempt. Ella sensed her frustration — why were they practising jumps when the kelpie was out there somewhere? Finally, Magpie refused a jump, so Ella took her over it one more time and called it a day. Who could concentrate, horse or girl, after everything that had happened?

If she stood in her stirrups, she could see Fiona still sitting in the circle, the magpies for company, along with a few finches that flitted around catching bugs. What was she doing there that had kept her occupied for so long?

Ella rode Magpie back to the yard, took off her saddle and gave her a drink. She patted her on the neck. 'Back soon, Maggie.'

Magpie ignored her. Was she in a mood? Or was she missing Olive?

As Ella neared the stone circle, she stopped. Fiona was singing, a low and sweet melody that sounded familiar. She drew closer, trying not to alert her sister. The song was in a language she didn't understand, but she recognised what it was — Scottish Gaelic. It was the same song she'd heard Grizzly singing on the shore of the lake that day — a slow and melancholic tune, full of longing and regret.

Fiona raised her head and stopped. Then she turned. For a moment her pale eyes looked through Ella as if she wasn't there — or as if she was there, but Fiona herself was somewhere else. Miles away. On the other side of the world, perhaps, beside another lake, a loch, lamenting her family.

But her eyes, sharp as ever, quickly drew focus.

'Oh,' she said. 'Hello.' As if slightly disappointed to see her.

'What are you doing?' Ella stepped into the circle.

There were holes in the dirt, and Grizzly's gardening trowel beside them, as though Fiona had been digging something up.

'I'm just making this,' Fiona said, and held up a rope, of sorts. She had braided together hay and straw, threaded through with flowers of red and blue and gold. The heady scent of spring was all around them.

'It's lovely,' said Ella. 'What is it? What's it for?'

'I'm going to catch the horse with it,' said Fiona. 'I'm going to use this.' She pulled something out of her pocket and held it out on her small, pale palm. It sat there, yellow, menacing. Ella wanted to hit it out of her hand. A tooth. Sharp and long. She'd seen those teeth before — though the memory was mizzly — in the jaws of a monster.

Fiona put the tooth back in her pocket and started humming — a sprightly tune this time, more suited to a jig than a funeral. She reached down beside her and picked up some feathers, fresh and sleek. Ella looked at the magpies, which had moved to the furthest stone, a safe distance. They looked away, furtive. *Did you give her those?* she thought.

She noticed for the first time that Fiona held a thick needle and thread, and was piercing the quills of the feathers and threading them into the rope. Craft was a skill she had learnt from Grizzly that had bypassed Ella.

'Well, let me know when you've finished it and we can give it to Mum and see if she can use it.' She was humouring her sister, she knew, but the work was keeping

Fiona occupied and in one place, so she was okay with that. 'I'm just going to the loo and to check on Grizzly, then I'll be in the yard with Magpie if you need me.'

Fiona nodded and kept on threading.

Grizzly was still on the couch, dozing. An uneaten sandwich sat on the table in front of her. Ella didn't need to check that she was breathing, because she was emitting a low, snuffly snore. She looked peaceful.

As she was washing her hands in the upstairs bathroom, Ella glanced out the window. The black horse stood in the middle of the stone circle.

One moment it hadn't been there, and the next it was there, its great shape like a black shadow sucking away all the light of the day. Fiona stood in front of it, holding out the rope she had made, bursting with flowers and feathers and now tied in a loose circle. The horse put its head down and allowed Fiona to guide it over its nose, eyes and ears to hang around its neck. Fiona's lips were moving, talking. Ella threw the window open and was about to yell when she realised she would startle the horse.

Fiona was in terrible, imminent danger.

'Get away, Fifi!' she said, but she knew it was too quiet. Neither horse nor girl looked at her; it was as if they were in each other's thrall.

With her heart pounding, Ella flung herself down the stairs and along the hallway to the back door. She threw it open.

Her stomach lurched.

Fiona, tiny Fiona, in her yellow raincoat, striped leggings and gumboots, was sitting astride the black horse, gripping the straw rope with one hand. The fingers of the other hand were laced into its mane.

The horse stood still, its head held high. Then it pawed the ground once, and looked at Ella. It was a look that said *catch me if you can*. Fiona slowly turned her face to Ella. Her pale eyes were wide, and contained a look of sheer, naked terror that Ella never wanted to see on her sister's face, ever.

Ella lunged forward, towards the stone circle, horse and child, but she knew it was too late. Even as she moved, the kelpie was already gathering its colossal muscles. With one movement, it leapt over the tallest stone and galloped away, Fiona a yellow speck on its great back.

'No!' Ella cried, and as she did so she heard an answering whinny from Magpie in the yard, and the magpies that had crowded around like a curiosity rose in the air as one and flew in pursuit, wheeling and pulsing through the sky.

Ella reacted instinctively. She ran back through the

house, calling, 'Grizzly! Grizzly! The horse has taken Fiona!'

Grizzly was groggy from sleep and struggled to sit up. 'Mother Earth save us!' she shouted, then, 'Take the shears from the bookcase, the iron shears. Go now, Ella, you're her only hope. Don't let them get to the lake.'

Ella didn't stop to think about what Grizzly wanted her to do with the shears — she didn't think if it came down to it she could kill the horse, or even wound it — but she ran to the bookcase and grabbed them. Her shoulder bag was beside the front door. She dropped the shears inside it and threw it over her head, so it banged against her back as she ran for the stable yard.

Magpie was waiting for her, head high, eyes wild. She'd broken the twine that tethered her lead rope, so Ella unclipped the rope from her halter and threw it to the ground. She pulled Magpie to the mounting block. There was no time to saddle her, but thank goodness she'd left her bridle on. She vaulted onto her bare back, and urged her through the open gate behind the house and in the direction Fiona and the horse had disappeared. Hoping, praying, that she wasn't too late.

But Magpie galloped harder than she'd ever done in her life. She knew exactly what was going on. *Save Fiona, save Fiona.* The words pounded in Ella's head along with the hoofbeats. When they came to the next gate, Ella didn't slow her down and Magpie didn't falter — they sailed over it.

'The magpies!' Ella yelled to her pony. 'Follow the magpies.'

She knew they wouldn't let her down. They showed her the direction Fiona and the kelpie had headed. And it wasn't directly towards the lake. The horse could have so easily made a beeline straight for the shore and taken them both into the water. Instead it headed south, along the track.

The fair. They were heading for the reserve where the whole community was gathered. What was the kelpie up to?

21

Morag looked at the line of children waiting to ride Peedie. She reckoned if it didn't get too much longer she could have a break soon and call Grizzly to make sure she and the girls were okay. The fair wasn't a huge event, not like some of the county fairs. It was more of a village fête: a welcome to spring, and a chance for children to see each other in the social drought of the holidays. It attracted a few tourists, so was good for the town's economy. There were stalls and competitions for the best vegetables, pies, jams and lambs. It was also a release after the freezing weather earlier in the week, and farmers stood around comparing livestock losses. No wonder they didn't want to help her, thought Morag. They had enough on their plates. Perhaps she had been too quick to attribute their indifference to her outcast status.

The reserve was next to the lakeside camping ground. It was the tamest spot in the area, with paddocks that were regularly mown, picnic tables and a toilet block, and a ramp for launching boats. There was a smaller artificial lake here too, which had created a safe swimming spot for families and was separated from the main lake by a dam of sorts.

A five-year-old girl called Hazel was astride the pony, a look of pure ecstasy on her face as Morag led her down the paddock to where the dry grass was tinged with white flowers.

'Do you think you want to have your own horse one day?' Morag asked, a question from her rather small repertoire of conversation starters she asked all the children. She had finally admitted to herself that she wasn't *good* with children who weren't her own.

'My mum says I can have one when I'm ten if I'm very good,' said Hazel. Morag smiled. That was literally a lifetime away for the poor child. She knew how privileged her girls were to have been around horses their whole lives, how coveted that life was by so many children. She could also see that many parents had been reluctant to let their children ride when they saw it was Morag who was taking them, but they had promised a pony ride, and hers was the only real one at the fair — she didn't count the creaking carousel with dead-eyed candy-coloured horses made from cheap plastic.

The fair was crowded. After the cold weather and the freak freeze, everybody seemed to have come out for the sunshine. Morag recognised families from the surrounding farms and smallholdings, as well as people from the town who worked in the tourist businesses or the salmon farms. Bunting lifted in the slight breeze; stalls overflowed with cakes and oversized vegetables, handmade knick-knacks and tooled leather bags.

A rickety ferris wheel wheezed around, and a bouncy castle shuddered under the weight of ten or so children throwing themselves against each other and shrieking. The carousel churned out maniacal accordion music and every now and then a loudspeaker sputtered into life to announce a lost child or the start of the next race — sack races, three-legged races and egg and spoon races. Despite the crowd, the mood was more subdued than Morag remembered; she supposed the disappearance of Josh Underhill was casting a pall over the usual excitement. The sky was huge above.

The artificial lake had become weedy over winter, and was tinted green. The rest of the lake was its usual dark blue, and the Ben, further away now, blended with the other mountains that, though distant, seemed to rise up from the water, topped with snow and wisped with cloud. It made the Basin feel enclosed, cut off from the outside world.

Morag gave an involuntary shudder.

Her thoughts went to Olive, and for a moment she saw an image of the mare swimming through the keld before sinking under the surface. How quickly she disappeared without a trace.

Peedie, with Hazel still on her back, reached the end of the paddock and turned back.

'Do you want to trot?' Morag asked. Hazel nodded, a thrill and terror on her face all at once. Morag clicked her tongue and started a slow jog. Peedie jogged along with her, smoother than your average trot. 'Hold on!' she said, and put one hand on Hazel's leg to stop her sliding off. Hazel squealed in delight.

Morag's mind went back even further then to that same spot in the lake where Olive had gone down. There she had come across Will's empty chair, his fishing rod and tackle box, his backpack with the thermos of tea still warm, and a half-eaten sandwich. The quad bike parked up off the track. She thought he'd just stepped away somewhere, but he'd been out all night. She knew how Josh's mother Susan felt all right. That not knowing was the worst.

She'd tried to shut out the things her mother had muttered, about it being Grizzly's fault, about the curse she'd brought with her that had taken first her husband, Morag's father, and then her son-in-law. And now Josh? And Olive? Had she imagined the black horse cantering across the surface of the water, willing Olive to follow it to her death? She must have. There was no explanation for it.

'There you go,' she said to Hazel, helping her dismount. Hazel's mother took the girl by the hand, mumbled a thanks without looking at Morag, and pulled her daughter away as she tried to get in a last pat of the pony's nose.

'Right,' said Morag. 'Who's next?'

As a small boy stepped nervously forward, something in the distance caught her eye — a small dark cloud, incongruous against the blue sky. It was moving towards them. It changed shape, became a flurry of sharp wings and bodies that grew ever bigger as more birds joined it. A mischief of magpies, moving as one. What were they up to?

The music from the carousel spluttered to an end, and then she heard it: hoofbeats. Someone was galloping a horse.

'Look!' someone shouted. People stopped what they were doing and looked towards the gentle hill that rose beyond the reserve. The black horse, cantering now, was moving along its crest. Its mane and tail flew behind it. It was magnificent. For a moment Morag felt the air go out of her body and the bodies of those around her. It was as if the whole fair was holding its breath to watch the spectacle. Even from here she could see the stallion's coat rippling in the sunshine, a deep black with a green sheen. But what was that? There was something around its neck and something on its back — or someone. It looked like a doll, perched like a jockey. The yellow of the figure's coat stood out starkly against the black.

A cry came up nearby, a woman's voice, stricken: 'It's a child!'

She was right. And not just any child. The yellow coat . . . it could only be. *Fiona*. Morag clutched at her throat. Her tiny precious baby, clinging on to the animal's mane for dear life. The horse slowed down for a moment, then reared, and pitched down the hill towards the fair.

The cloud of magpies moved with it, high in the air.

MAGPIE'S BODY WAS hot beneath Ella, who held on with her legs, reins high up the neck, disengaging her mind and her fears as they galloped over the paddocks, scattering sheep and lambs. Magpie soared bravely over gates, higher than she'd ever jumped before. They couldn't see the horse with Fiona on its back, save the odd flash of yellow, and for once Ella was grateful that Fiona never took off that stupid coat.

It was the magpies that guided them. All the words for a flock of magpies passed through Ella's mind on a loop, in time with her pony's hoofbeats drumming the earth: *mischief, murder, parliament, congregation, conventicle, tribe, charm.* The cloud of birds grew bigger as more and more birds joined it, until it was a murmuration, waving like a big black flag in the sky, saying, *Here they are! Follow, follow!*

The stallion couldn't be going at a gallop. They were gaining on it, so it must have slowed to a languid canter, taunting them — she'd never thought of a horse as arrogant before, but then this wasn't really a horse, was it? She had to keep reminding herself of that fact. She saw Gus's superior face, sneering at her.

In the distance there was a commotion, a hot jumble of colour — the fair. They were definitely headed for the reserve. But why?

As they crested the hill overlooking the lake, Ella pulled Magpie up to take stock and to try to work out what the kelpie would do next. There was a stillness about the fair she hadn't expected. The ferris wheel was not churning, though there were people on it, perched and swaying in a carriage at the top. The only movement was the flutter of bunting; it was as though the whole event had been trapped in amber: the people stood straight and unmoving, transfixed by the sight of the horse with Fiona on its back. It cantered around the perimeter of the fairground, tail held high and streaming behind it. Ella recognised the movement it was making — it had done it in her dream, with the horses in the paddock, and it had done it with Olive on the shore of the lake. Was it herding everyone, or weaving a spell?

From her vantage point, she scanned the reserve for her mother. *There.* In a small grassed area, staked out with a homepainted sign hanging off a gate: PONY RIDES $2. Morag appeared to be frozen along with everyone else, holding the lead rope of the little Shetland pony. Peedie pranced beside her on his short stumpy legs. All faces were turned towards the horse.

Ella had to think fast. She urged Magpie on, and they plunged down the hill. Her bag, holding the iron shears, thumped at her back.

At the perimeter of the reserve she slowed Magpie to a fast walk.

'Someone help that poor girl!' shouted a woman at a salmon stall who Ella recognised as her classmate Miriama McLeod's mother. 'She's terrified!'

Ella turned Magpie to meet the horse head on. It was cantering anti-clockwise — she would go in the other direction. All her instincts were telling her not to, to be afraid and to ride away instead, but for once she resisted her impulse. She had to save her sister.

As they approached the calm artificial lake, Ella glimpsed tiny boats, and men and children standing ankle deep in the water, staring, while their remote-controlled vessels veered around them. She saw the cloud of magpies first, then heard the rumbling hooves of the kelpie as it reached the shore, where she and Magpie were blocking its path. It slowed to a walk. Fiona, her hand still tangled in its mane, was crying, her mouth twisted in a terrible knot.

'Ellie?' she wailed. 'I'm sorry. I thought it would listen to me.'

'Fi,' called Ella. 'I know it's high, and scary, but now that it's stopped can you jump down?'

Magpie skittered beneath her, tossing her head. The kelpie came to a complete stop, lifted its head and bellowed. It was not the sound of a horse. It was the sound of crashing water, or lowing beasts, of rocky shores in a storm. It peeled its lips back in a sneer and Ella glimpsed those terrible teeth, sharp and stained.

'I'm stuck!' called Fiona. She lifted her slight shoulders. 'My hand's stuck in its mane, like glue — I'm scared, Ellie!'

The magpies above took their moment and swooped, attacking the horse's head. It reared and tossed its great skull back and forth. The sound of bird wings became deafening, a flurry like an avalanche. Through it, Fiona screamed.

'Stop!' Ella yelled at the birds. 'Please!' Her greatest fear was that the horse would turn and plunge into the lake, taking Fiona with it. Or that Fiona would fall with her hand still tangled in the mane and be trampled under its hooves, or maimed between its sharp jaws.

The birds listened, and to Ella's astonishment rose away. It was too late for one of them. The kelpie spat the magpie out of its mouth, and it landed, bloody, on the ground between them. A challenge.

The air stilled. The only sound was her own breath. The kelpie raised one front hoof and pawed the ground.

A deep rumbling came from across the lake. Behind the mountains rose a great black cloud. It came rushing across the Basin, eclipsing the blue sky, covering the sun that had been warming the spring day. A howl rose up from around the fair and beyond. Dogs: sheep dogs and pets, their voices calling — sharp, frightened, worshipful. Up on the distant hills sheep rushed to flock together; they moved as one, back and forth.

Soon the valley was as dark as twilight. The Ben appeared to grow taller, to stretch and groan above them, but it was only the clouds making it appear bigger. It was as though a lid had been put on the Basin and there was no escape for anyone, human or animal.

22

Ella edged closer, feeling the weight of the shears in the bag at her back. If she could get between the kelpie and the lake, Fiona might have a chance.

She leaned slightly to the left and gave a flick of her pelvis. Magpie felt the subtlety of the gesture and started to move forward and to the left, tossing her head.

The kelpie's eyes burned into them. It was waiting, blowing great gusts out its dark nostrils.

'It's okay, Fi,' she called, trying to reassure her terrified sister.

'Ella? What's going on?' Magpie came to a halt as Morag appeared beside them and put one hand on Ella's leg. The other she held palm up, towards the horse.

At the sound of her voice the kelpie snorted. Then it wheeled on its back legs and paced away, not towards the

lake, as Ella expected it to, but into the fair. It stepped
high, then broke into a canter.

'Mummy!' cried Fiona. The sound sliced into
Ella's skin.

'Fi!' Morag called back.

The horse swept past a mother and child, throwing
up a spray of mud that spattered them like blood.
A nightmare unfolded, with its own terrible logic: the
little girl was suddenly astride the kelpie's back and the
mother was staring in disbelief at the spot where she'd
been standing. The girl, now behind Fiona, twisted to
look at her mother as the horse cantered away. A look of
uncanny delight had settled on the child's face.

At that, the stillness erupted. The mother screamed
the girl's name: 'Anahera!'

Morag took off in pursuit and Ella didn't wait to
be told; she urged Magpie into the kelpie's wake as it
rampaged through the fairground. It veered close to a
table of jams; the table tipped, and glass jars scattered.
It tore through a string of bunting, which got caught
on its neck and trailed absurdly behind, colourful flags
flying.

Another child, a blond boy, appeared on the kelpie's
back and wrapped his arms around Anahera, and then
another, older this time, who Ella recognised as Sylvie

O'Regan from school. The girl raised one fist in the air and let out a whoop.

To the children, the kelpie was just another fairground ride. Their faces and bodies showed no fear; this was adventure, pure adrenaline. As the kelpie reached the outer edges of the reserve it veered around towards the tractor displays. A small green-jacketed, dark-haired boy launched himself from where he was standing on top of a tractor. Sylvie caught him and helped him settle behind her.

There were now five children on the horse's back — now another, a tiny thing, smaller than Fiona. *Six* children. It was impossible.

Ella pulled Magpie to a stop next to where Morag stood with her hands on her knees, puffing, by the ferris wheel. She had a terrible thought that the kelpie might knock it over; there were still people in it, trapped at the top, rocking in their carriage. As if in answer, it creaked like a ghost.

'Oh my god,' said Morag, straightening and pointing. 'It's growing. It's getting bigger.'

She was right. The kelpie's back was somehow able to accommodate each new child. It was cantering with its head and tail held high, coming back towards Ella and Morag now, but it left the ferris wheel alone and thundered past. Parents, farmers, fairground officials — all looked helplessly on, either unsure what to do or physically unable to move.

There were eight children on the kelpie's back now. Fiona was soaking wet, miserably clinging on to its dripping mane, while the children behind her laughed and hollered, having the time of their lives.

'I can't watch this,' said Morag. Her face was white. 'I have to do something.'

She ran after the horse, anticipating where it was going to turn, and moved to cut it off. She stood in its path and raised her hands towards it.

'Whoa, the horse,' she called in a low voice, but Ella knew it was useless. She was talking to the kelpie as if it was a horse, but this creature was something else. It had its own rules. Morag seemed to realise this as she stood there.

'No more children!' she called. 'You've done enough! Let them go.'

The kelpie stopped in front of her, stamping at the ground. It let out a piercing squeal that filled the gloomy sky. Morag was joined by another parent, and then another — the people had awoken from their paralysis. A man Ella recognised as a young farmer, a champion sheep shearer, appeared beside Morag, clutching a rope. He murmured something in her ear, and Morag nodded.

The man held the rope out from his body; it was tied in a loop. Was he going to try and lasso the horse? Ella watched on, anxious. It would never work. Could it?

One of the children yelled out, 'Go, horsey, go!' They were still oblivious to the danger they were in: beglamoured. All except Fiona, who had shut down now. She was slumped forward, her face awry, both her hands now tangled in the wet mane. The straw rope was still around the kelpie's neck, but it was tatty, shredded. Its power was gone.

The man began to swing his rope, first at his side and then above his head. The rope formed a small tornado, and as it turned Ella pinned hope onto it — hope that it would fly through the air, snare the kelpie, and the children would be saved. But her hopes were mortal. They should have known a kelpie couldn't be caught by human methods.

The loop left the man's hand and found its mark, but when it landed, high up on the kelpie's neck, it melted away like butter and fell to the ground. The kelpie tossed its head, and Ella had the distinct feeling it was laughing at them. It lurched forward, spun around and kicked out with a massive hind leg. Its hoof caught the man in the chest and he went flying back into Morag. The two of them sprawled in the dirt.

'Mum!' Ella sprang to the ground. Morag rolled herself from beneath the farmer, who was gasping for breath, winded. He clutched his chest, his face screwed up in pain.

The kelpie, triumphant, gave another wretched whinny and took off towards the lake.

Morag got up. 'I'm fine,' she said. 'Ella, go! Magpie is the only chance we have. Be brave, my love, go!'

Ella didn't need any more coaxing. She threw herself onto Magpie's back as though she had been lifted by the wind, and the two of them, girl and pony, raced after the monster with the children on its back. She must not fail. This was their last chance. Holding the reins with one hand, she reached behind her and into the bag. She drew out the iron shears and held them at the ready.

The kelpie was not moving as quickly now; the weight of the children and its uncanny proportions were slowing it down. It bypassed the shallow pool, scattering a group of parents who were holding a blanket between them — as if they planned to stop it that way — and headed straight for the main lake, which was inky black and eerily calm, the sky above pressing down like basalt.

The kelpie entered the water and slowed to a lazy lope, taunting them, gliding out on the lake's surface. Magpie stopped in the shallows and pawed at the water. The kelpie swung around and stopped, looking at them, daring them to follow it into the depths.

What could Ella do? If Fiona was stuck, did that mean the rest of the children were too? If they jumped now, the lake was surely not too deep and they could swim to shore.

She called out. 'Jump!'

The children suddenly looked uncertain. Sylvie, who was the oldest, seemed to wake from a dream; she gazed around, blinking. She took in the lake, and the horse standing on its surface, and the children in front of and behind her, and confusion and fear flickered over her face.

'Ella!' she called. 'What's happening? Help!'

'Can you jump? Can you get down and help the other children off?'

At that moment the kelpie side-stepped and tossed its head.

'I can't!' yelled Sylvie. 'I'm stuck!'

The other children, aware now of the danger they were in, started to wail. They too squirmed desperately but they were stuck fast.

Ella urged Magpie further into the water. They would swim if they had to.

But they didn't have to swim. There was lightness in Magpie's step, the shallow splash of hooves in a puddle. Ella looked down past Magpie's sweat-flecked shoulder, past her own legs clinging to the hot piebald coat.

Magpie was walking on the water.

There was no time to absorb the shock. Ella urged her pony to canter, and then they were flying across the surface, making barely a sound. Ella readied the shears.

She wasn't going to kill it, was she?

Instinct took over, and Magpie slowed as she approached the kelpie with her head held high. Perhaps it was stunned, curious, but it didn't move. It watched on, even took an uncertain step backward. The two horses arched their necks and blew into each other's nostrils. On the water, in its element now, the kelpie's skin, away from land, had turned hairless and slate grey, like an eel's, with a cool green shimmer. It shone, viscous, in the dull light, reflected the oppressive black clouds. The children's legs were smeared with slime.

Suddenly, it reared and struck out, missing Magpie's head by centimetres. It pulled back its lips in a leer, showing its monstrous teeth.

'Gus!' Ella screamed. 'It's me! *Please*. Let them go.'

There was no trace left of the boy with the cheeky grin. The boy whose voice had said her name, that had sounded like bells and skylarks and sunlight falling through water. In front of her was a monster.

But she saw it hesitate. Something shifted in its tawny eyes, and for a moment Ella saw herself reflected in them. Gus had to be in there somewhere. A part of the kelpie surely had to remember that they had once been friends, no matter how shallow, how manipulative that friendship had been. They had laughed together. There *had* to be something still there.

In that moment, Magpie swung her body sideways and Ella saw what she needed to do. She reached up and grabbed Fiona's arm with one hand, while brandishing the iron shears with the other.

'Hold still, Fi,' she whispered.

23

The shears sliced through the kelpie's mane with a hissing sound, and Fiona shook free of the strands that had bound her, watching them fall away. She grabbed the remains of the tattered straw rope and swung herself down onto Magpie's back.

'Quick!' said Ella to Anahera. 'Jump on!' But the terrified child shook her head, reached forward and grabbed the kelpie's mane, sealing her fate and that of the children behind her.

Before Ella could do anything more, the kelpie stirred. It let out an almighty howl. Its tail solidified and snaked behind it, twisting into a scaly point. It threw up its terrible head and bared its teeth. *We're done for*, thought Ella, and cowered, while Fiona held tightly to her waist.

But instead of attacking, it reared one last time, bounded into a gallop across the surface of the lake with the screaming children on its back, and then plunged into the depths.

The kelpie and the children were gone.

The solid dark clouds rolled back as quickly as they had come, revealing a thin grey wash. Fiona reached into her pocket and pulled out the kelpie's tooth. She drew back her arm and threw as hard as she could in the direction it had dived.

Magpie, with Ella and Fiona on her back, sank slowly into the water and began swimming. It wasn't long before her hooves reached solid ground. But there on the lakeshore, all was chaotic and upsetting. Adults and children huddled on the shore; some of the parents of the taken children were on their knees, wailing, while others had rushed into the water, screaming their names. Behind them, the fair was a jumble of knocked-over tables and untethered bunting; the bouncy castle was a collapsed balloon and a tent had caught fire — someone was spraying it with a hose. Two men pushed jet-skis into the water; the engines juddered into life and they zoomed out onto the lake, searching.

Morag ran through the water towards her daughters and grabbed Magpie's bridle. Her face was grim and tear-streaked. Without speaking, she reached for Fiona, who circled her arms around her mother's neck, burying her face as she slipped silently off the horse's back. Morag put her hand briefly on Ella's knee and nodded, sadness and grief etched on her face, but also relief. It could have been so much worse. She could have been one of the parents on the shore, keening, pulling at their clothes in anguish.

'I'm going to put Fiona in the ute,' Morag said. 'I'll bring you a blanket.' She always kept blankets for spontaneous picnics, for an unexpected chill. Fiona, still wearing her bright yellow coat, curled into her. Ella wanted to follow, for them all just to climb into the ute and go home, close the door, wish the world away.

Instead, she nodded. 'And a towel for Magpie?'

'A towel, and anything she wants, for life. I mean it. She saved our Fiona.' Morag didn't smile; she was dead serious. 'I don't know what she is, and it doesn't matter. I don't want to know. She's your pony, and that's enough.' She turned and carried Fiona away.

Ella slid off Magpie and leaned into her while she took in the crowd on the beach — the confusion, the despair. A figure stood at the back, watching her. She sensed before she saw that it was Susan, Josh's mother. There was no malice in her look. She was just staring, as if Ella and Magpie held all the answers to everyone's questions, and she was the only one who knew it.

Ella shivered under her wet clothes. Her teeth chattered and she willed Morag to return with the blanket. She moved so she couldn't see Susan looking at her. She had no doubt now that Josh had been taken by the kelpie and drowned in the lake, along with the rest of the children. It hit her then, and she buried her face in Magpie's mane and cried hot tears. Magpie bent her neck and blew warm air on the back of Ella's legs, comforting her in her own way.

She had to leave the beach. She wiped her eyes on her wet sleeve, tugged on Magpie's reins and led her up the grassy bank to where water troughs were laid out for the show animals. Magpie drank long and deep, making slurping noises. From here, Ella could see down over the beach, at the parents collapsed on the rocky sand, crying, or now in boats desperately searching the water. It hurt that she hadn't been able to save the children. She felt it deep within her body, a wailing, an aching wind inside her veins — worse than she felt when her father died, because she had tried to save them, and she had failed.

Out over the lake, the sky was a thick, dull grey. The water was glassy, a black, impenetrable mirror that reflected the Ben and the other hills around. A silence rose off it like steam, then a mizzle of rain began to fall, a weeping sky, and Ella turned her face up to it.

Something caught her eye up on the ridge. A slight figure on a quad bike turned and tore down the slope. A red bush shirt. Gumboots. No helmet. Its head was crowned by a flame of white hair, streaming behind as the bike made its way to the reserve. It disappeared out of sight, just as Morag came up behind Ella with a blanket and a towel.

'Fiona's asleep in the front seat,' she said. 'She's exhausted. But warm and dry. I had to take her coat off which didn't please her very much.' She laid a hand on Ella's shoulder, then pulled her into an embrace. 'Here.' She wrapped the blanket around her and drew it tight. Then she threw the towel over Magpie's neck and began rubbing it. Magpie let her, which was a miracle. Morag had never been able to get near her. Maybe she sensed that something momentous had happened — that they were all in it together.

'Come on,' said Morag. 'Let's go home. We'll put Magpie in the float with Peedie.'

'I can ride her—'

'No arguments. I'm not having you riding home while you're still wet and cold. We need to be together. And we need to check on Grizzly. I don't like leaving her alone, not right now.'

Magpie resisted. She pulled back from the ramp. Her ears were pricked, alert, and she kept turning towards the lake.

'Come on, *please*, Maggie,' said Ella. 'There's nothing we can do right now.'

Finally, Magpie relented and rushed up the ramp, nearly bowling Ella over.

They had just finished shutting the float door when the sound of an engine made Ella turn. The quad bike had made its way down to the shore. It bumped and skidded over stones, then stopped.

Morag turned then too. 'Is that—?' she gasped.

It was Grizzly. Sick, frail Grizzly. Perched on top of the quad bike with a red bush shirt over her white night-dress, her feet shoved into gumboots that made her legs look as thin as chicken bones. Her white hair cascaded, loose, down her back.

'What is she doing?' asked Ella.

Morag's mouth was set in a grim line. 'She can't be here. Oh my god. That's all we need. Let's go.'

As they hurried down the bank towards her, Grizzly got off the quad bike, clutching her walking stick. She was wobbly on her legs, like a newborn foal. For a moment she stooped over, but she said something quietly to herself and stood up straight, a look of fierce determination on her face. Here was the Grizzly they knew, not the fragile creature of a moment ago.

Nobody on the shore had noticed her. They were too busy looking out at the lake. Parents held each other. The children left behind clutched their hands, put their arms around their legs and leaned into them. Some of them had lost brothers and sisters. Grizzly weaved her way through them, looking at everyone in disbelief. Ella saw her put a hand on a shoulder, whisper a word to someone who recoiled from her but gestured to the lake. Grizzly nodded grimly. She staggered on through the people, who moved out of her way, watching her silently.

She reached the shore and with great effort put one foot on a large flat rock. She hoisted her walking stick up and used it to pull herself all the way. Then she stood tall again and planted her feet. She raised her arms, and the walking stick, above her head and called out, 'Aonghas Donn!'

Her voice was cracked and quiet, and a few of the people on the shore nudged each other and turned away. Just that crazy old witch trying to take all the attention, calling to her friend.

'Is she delirious? What's she doing?' Morag asked

nobody in particular. She and Ella were getting nearer. They could see the cracks in Grizzly's face, the sores that marked her thin, purple- veined legs. And something else that Ella glimpsed as Grizzly raised her arms again and called out in a clear, loud voice:

'*Aonghas Donn!*'

A knife, strapped to her thigh. Because she never went swimming without her knife.

'Mum, what are you doing?' called Morag. She was by the rock now, stepping up onto it, grabbing Grizzly's elbow, with Ella close behind. 'Let me take you home.'

'No!' Grizzly shouted, and snatched her arm away.

The crowd on the beach had fallen silent, and the people in boats were drifting in from the water. Everyone turned to watch, waiting, sensing that something important was happening.

'Stay back!'

Morag did what she was told and took a few steps back, stumbling off the edge of the rock and righting herself in the sand. She glanced uncertainly at Ella. Then a small, warm hand slipped into hers. Fiona was beside her, wrapped in a blanket, quietly watching.

'Fi?' said Morag.

Her youngest child looked up at her. 'She knows what she's doing, Mum.'

Morag just nodded. Hot tears prickled at Ella's eyes; she didn't know why. Something about the sight of her mother, stilled, held by her tiny child, while Grizzly, so diminished but full of fire, stood looking out to the lake.

'It's me he wants. This is all my fault. I brought him here, and only I can send him away.'

'Mum, what are you talking about?' But Fiona squeezed Morag's hand and she fell silent.

'He doesn't belong here. I told you, he's come to this country and taken what is not his. I am going to send him back. I told you I would fix things.' And she raised her arms again, swinging her walking cane, higher this time, and shouted out once more.

'Aonghas Donn! You've got my attention now — is that no' what you wanted? So come and take me, ye great wretch of a creature. Leave these folk alone!'

Ella couldn't let Grizzly face the kelpie on her own. She stepped up on the rock to stand next to her. Grizzly lowered her arms and took Ella by the hand. Ella looked into her eyes, and from their crinkly, hooded shells Grizzly's eyes looked back, giving her the courage she needed. She turned her face to the lake.

'Gus!' Ella shouted. 'Come out, you coward, you monster!'

A great peal of thunder rolled across the sky from one end of the Basin to the other.

Were they really going to ask him to come back out, to show himself once more? But Ella just knew that Grizzly was sure of what she was doing. She had to trust her.

As the rumbling continued, the still black water of the lake began to shudder, blurring the reflection of the mountains. An unfriendly stour-wind tore up the valley, lifting Grizzly's hair and driving the cold into their bones. White caps appeared on the surface of the lake. Then, it began to boil. Above, the clouds boiled as well. The landscape was alive.

The people on the shore huddled together, fearful of a great storm that bubbled out of nowhere.

Out in the lake, in the keld, something broke the surface of the water. A dark shape emerged, like a mountain. It rose up, up, up towards the sky. It was black as obsidian, and like a black hole it sucked all the meagre light and joy out of the world. A child, somewhere, wailed. Ella's heart hammered; she felt blood pumping through her skin, her organs, around her body. She remembered what Gus had said to her: *They can hear your blood tinkling in your veins. That's how a kelpie hunts, you know.*

The black mountain swelled ever larger, the back of a giant creature. Waterfalls poured off its sides, which shimmered green with moss. It towered above them. Finally, out of the water, a head emerged. It was the giant head of a horse and not a horse. It was something ancient and terrible, with eyes full of pain and anger.

Then the screaming began. All around them, the people from the fair tore through the sand, some falling onto their hands and knees and climbing up again. Throwing themselves onto the bank to escape, to get as far from the lake and the terrible sight as they could.

Grizzly squeezed Ella's hand and turned to her.

'I've got the shears, Grizzly, like you told me. They cut through its mane. I saved Fiona. We can do it.' Ella's voice sounded more sure than she was herself.

'You're a brave lass,' said Grizzly. 'I'm so proud of you. But now you have to do something even braver.'

'Anything,' said Ella, though she didn't feel brave inside. But isn't that what courage is after all? Being afraid but doing it anyway? She could do this. Together they could face the kelpie.

'You have to let me go now, Ella.'

'What? No.'

The creature opened its mouth with its dripping, yellow teeth, and roared. A hot wind blasted over the lake, knocking over everyone left on the beach, carrying with it the stink of fish and fire. The sound was deafening. It was met by another roll of thunder in the roiling sky.

Ella jumped up and pulled Grizzly back to her feet.

Once standing, Grizzly wrenched her hands away. 'Go,' she said. 'This is how you can save everyone, don't you see? Your sister, your ma. Everyone. You have to let me go and face the kelpie on my own. I brought him here, and only I can send him away. I am going to die and you have to let me do this.'

For a moment Ella saw the old Grizzly, sun-tough and capable of anything, and then the young Griselda, strong and black-haired and determined. Then she nodded.

A sob escaped her as she backed away. *It's the only way. She was always going to die, you just didn't accept it.*

She left the rock to stand close beside Morag and Fiona.

Grizzly's arms were stiff by her sides and she looked over at her family. Her determined expression was fading. Swithering, she would have said.

'Grizzly?' Ella called out. The question hung in the air.

Grizzly nodded. 'Aye,' she answered, and shifted the grip on her walking stick. 'Get back now, further.' The uncertainty in her face vanished and she turned back to the lake, while Morag pulled the girls further away. Ella could feel, through her mother's trembling hands, that she was swithering too. It was a huge effort for Morag to leave her mother standing alone.

'Come on then!' Grizzly cried. 'Are you feart or what?'

Then the creature began to move. It came towards them from out of the deep, walking. And as it came, it began to shrink. It strained against the force of the water and grew smaller with every step. It began to change shape as well. Its bulk refined; its head became less monster and more horse; a mane sprouted from its neck. Finally, it stood before them, on the surface of the lake. Arched neck. The black stallion. The kelpie. It regarded Grizzly, but it also took in Morag, and Fiona, and Ella, almost greedily. Ella thought again of how arrogant it seemed.

The sky became still, and the surface of the water was again dark and glassy. Through the enveloping silence, Ella heard the beating of wings. A cloud of magpies hovered: waiting, witnessing. And somewhere a distant scream and a thud. Magpie, in the horse float, hammering to get out.

'If it's me you want,' called Grizzly, 'then come and get me!'

The horse tossed its head and high-stepped forward, over the water and up the shore to where Grizzly waited on the rock, her arms by her sides. She tossed her walking stick aside and raised her palms out as if in reassurance. The horse hesitated, then walked on, picking its way over the rocky sand until it was standing before her. She was small and insignificant beside it, even on the rock. Ella felt Morag stiffen beside her and draw in a sharp breath; she was fighting every instinct not to run forward and intervene.

'It's okay, Mum,' said Fiona, reassuring. 'Just watch.'

The horse lowered its head towards Grizzly and nuzzled her stomach. Grizzly responded by smacking it across the nose, as she would with one of the trekking horses that tried to nip her.

Surprised, the horse stumbled back, then reared. When it came down, it flickered and became the shape of a man briefly before resuming its equine form. Ella gasped. The man had been young, slender, an older version of the boy she recognised. He'd had weeds in his hair.

Grizzly shouted something in Gaelic that they couldn't understand. Her voice was full of anger and grief. The horse went very still, admonished. It stepped forward gingerly and lowered its head again.

Ella knew then, deep within her bones, that the kelpie couldn't help its nature any more than the Ben could help its rockiness, or magpies their meddling, or wolves their hunting instinct. It was of the lake and the earth, and it had always been alive in its intangible, incomprehensible place, but it was not of this country. It was time for it to go.

And because it was outside time, her family had always been connected to it — for who knew how many generations? — and to the ancient force that had brought it here to stand on the shore of this lake at the bottom of the world.

And Ella finally understood. Without sacrifice, the curse of the kelpie was destined to repeat itself, without end, down generations. And somehow everyone in the Basin had also been destined to play their part.

On the rock, Grizzly took the kelpie's great head in her hands and pressed her face to its forehead. She closed her eyes. They stood like that for a long time while the world stood still and watched. Then, opening her eyes, she looked at her daughter and granddaughters.

'I'm sorry,' she called. 'I love you all.' And with that, she was flying through the air, leaping like a child onto the horse's back, kicking off her boots.

'No!' screamed Morag, and darted forward.

The horse reared in triumph, pivoted in the sand, and took off at a gallop, its hooves ringing on rocks. Grizzly crouched low over its neck, holding its mane with only one hand, her skinny legs and feet white against its hide. With the other hand, she reached to her thigh, and drew the knife that was strapped there. As the horse galloped across the surface of the water, she held it high, piercing the sky. But before anyone could see what happened next, the kelpie dived below the surface. They were gone. The lake and sky bubbled and then went still.

24

Morag sank to her knees, and Ella followed, a hollow chasm opening up inside her. She reached out her arms to encircle her mother and sister, and Morag reached back. Fiona, in her blanket, was cocooned between them.

'What has she done?' whispered Morag through her tears.

'She's saved us,' Fiona said, then was jerked by a small sob. 'She saved us from the kelpie, Mum. I thought I could keep us safe, but it was Grizzly all along.'

Morag buried her face in her children's hair. Ella looked out at the lake, seeing the still water. It was true then. Grizzly was gone. But so was the kelpie, and this time it was forever.

Along the shore, the people who had fled the sight of the kelpie started to come back. The family huddle was repeated down the beach as families of the taken children cried together, comforting each other. Nobody knew what else to do, what else could be done. They stared out into the lake. They stole glances at Grizzly's family, so many questions no doubt forming about what they had witnessed. But they kept their distance.

The clouds drifted apart, and the spring sun shone down. Grizzly would have a word for that: a nature word, with a double meaning.

Morag let out a sigh and wiped her cheeks on her sleeve. Ella turned her face to the sun and felt its warmth. She wondered how much her mother understood about what had happened, because surely, as Grizzly's daughter, she would feel it in her bones as Ella did. Feel the pull down the years, a line of girls and women stretching back to the beginning of time. Or perhaps Ella's relationship with Gus, with the kelpie itself, had given her more clarity than Morag had — it had at last allowed her to tidy some of the jumble in that house in her head. Fiona knew. Ella reached out and squeezed her hand. Fiona probably knew more than she did.

They stood up and brushed themselves down, feeling stiff and sore. Beside them, the lake was frilled by tiny waves, which shushed quietly against the stones. A bigger wave rolled in, as though caused by the wake of a passing boat, but the lake was deserted now. The jet-skis and kayaks had returned to shore.

'Something's happening to the lake,' said Fiona. Nobody else seemed to have noticed. But she was right. The water was beginning to ruffle as it did in a Nor'wester, with little white caps — white horses, they always called them — though the day remained still.

Then a small wave washed up the beach and they had to back away quickly to avoid getting doused. A child squealed, and people down the shoreline leapt to their feet. The first wave was followed by another, bigger this time, and suddenly everyone was bending down to gather up their things to get away from the water, scrambling up the bank.

Then, impossibly, from the middle of the lake there came a great blue wave topped with white, followed by another, and another. Afterwards, everyone would remember the waves shaped like white horses that came out of nowhere. They could have sworn they saw the elegant noses and milky manes, sharp eyes and galloping legs as the water formations moved swiftly towards them over the surface of the lake. For a moment the horses were suspended above the shore, tossing their heads, while the people looked on with fear and excitement and utter disbelief. But today was a day for believing in impossible things.

The waves crashed down onto the beach, one after

the other. And just as quickly as they had come, the horses disappeared, receded, sluicing the stones with a chatter. The water was still. The crowd was silent, watching as one from the safety of the bank.

'Look!' someone shouted. And they looked.

The waves had left behind what looked like sodden piles of clothes. Ella counted them: seven. But already Fiona had broken away and was running down the bank towards the closest pile. Morag grabbed at the space between them and called Fiona's name.

The little girl reached the dark shape before Morag and Ella had roused themselves to follow. She crouched down and turned it over. She squealed and looked up, her face unreadable — fear, relief, worry.

'It's Anahera!' she cried. 'Mum, it's Anahera.'

'Oh god,' Morag whispered, and ran towards her youngest daughter, calling out for Anahera's mother. Ella followed.

Up and down the beach, the people had flooded back and had fallen on the other shapes on the sand.

Fiona, Morag and Ella were kneeling beside Anahera when she opened her eyes and gasped. She coughed. Her dark hair was slicked back and her clothes sodden. Morag crouched down and lifted the girl's head gently, scooping her arm under her to lift her up.

'You right, love? Are you okay? Can you speak?'

Anahera's face was still pale with shock, but she nodded. 'I think so,' she whispered. 'Yes, I'm okay.'

'It's a miracle,' said Morag, as the sand thumped beside them and they heard Anahera's mother scream her name. Morag leaned aside as the mother grabbed Anahera and, sobbing, held her close, rocking her back and forth like a baby. Fiona took off her blanket and gave it to them.

'Thank you,' said Anahera's mother, and she looked each of them in the eyes. Ella knew they were being thanked for so much more than a blanket. There had been seven piles on the beach, one for each child taken.

The children were gathered in their parents' arms and moved away from the shore, from the scene of the devastation. As Ella and her family joined the exodus, she looked back. There was a lone figure left standing on the sand. Ella had seen Susan, Josh's mother, walking along the beach, stopping at every child, her arms folded protectively over her body and a hope on her face that diminished as she went. Now she was joined by her husband, who put his arm around her shoulder and tried to coax her away from the shore. She shook her head and stood her ground, grim and determined, looking out at the lake.

'Come on,' said Morag. 'We need to check on the ponies. I feel like we should be getting home, but . . .'

She didn't need to say it. Grizzly wasn't there. There was no point.

But as Ella turned to go, another wave began forming in the middle of the lake. It rose up silently and glided towards the shore, shining in the late-afternoon sun. Susan and her husband scrambled up the bank and sat down to watch.

It rose up and once again took the form of a white horse, but when it reached the shore, and the wave receded, the white horse remained. Standing on the beach, her head down, was Olive.

'Mum—' Ella grabbed her mother's hand.

'I don't believe it,' Morag said.

Olive wasn't alone. A figure was on her back, slumped forward, its head on her mane and its arms around her neck. Dark and dripping wet.

Susan ran forward, shouting something incomprehensible. Her husband was close behind and together they fell on the figure, wrapping their arms around it and pulling it to the ground, crying.

Josh.

His father bent and picked him up. Josh's face was white in the pale light. But he was alive. Ella saw him

279

blink, once, twice, then nod, before laying his head on his father's shoulder.

Relief flooded through her, but it was tempered by the knowledge that all of this, somehow, was still her fault. That she had invited the kelpie into their lives that night when she had stood at her window, in its sight, and wished for a friend. That she had cursed Josh Underhill that day, and even if she didn't really hold the power to curse anyone, the kelpie had heard her words and it had acted on them. Phrases came to her now — *watch your back* and *be careful what you wish for*.

Morag was beside Olive, checking her over, running her hands over her legs, scanning for injuries. Ever the practical one. Fiona stood at Olive's bowed head, rubbing and rubbing at her neck. The mare's saddle and bridle had gone; she glowed white on the shore. Her clean emergence from the lake reminded Ella of a rebirth.

Morag began walking up the wide path to the bank, with her hand on Olive's neck. The horse followed eagerly, stepping soundly.

'At least some people have had their happy ending,' Morag said as she approached. 'And we have our Olive back. Come on, let's get going.'

'Wait,' said Fiona. 'There's somebody else.'

They looked towards the shore again, past where

Josh and Olive had washed up. Fiona was right. There was another shape. Not just a pile of clothes. This shape slowly sat up and turned over to crouch on its hands and knees, head hanging, breathing heavily. Then it planted one foot on the sand, then the other, and rose shakily. This was no child. This was a man.

'No,' breathed Morag. 'It can't be.'

'Mum?' said Fiona uncertainly.

But Morag was gone. She had broken into a run and was sprinting down the bank, slipping and falling and getting back up again. She ran to stand in front of the man. The two of them stared at each other for a moment. And then Morag threw herself at him, threw her arms around his neck, and the two of them stood there in a long, slow embrace.

'Who is it?' said Fiona, turning her face to Ella.

But Ella was already moving. She turned and grabbed Fiona by the hand, pulling her.

'It's Dad,' said Ella. 'Our dad!' And together they ran down onto the waiting shore.

25

*Glisk: a fleeting glimpse of sunlight
through cloud; a flash of hope in
the heart*

It was collective, retrospective amnesia. Nobody except
Ella and her family remembered the events of that day,
and life carried on in the Basin as usual. According to
Josh's parents, they could only recall wandering down
from the fair to find their son sitting on the beach,
unharmed but unable to tell them what had happened
to him. To the other parents and children, or so they
claimed, there had been some unusual weather patterns
that day, which had produced some unusual waves on
the lake, but the kelpie never existed, never dragged the
children down into the depths of the lake before finally
releasing them.

But for Ella, Morag and Fiona, the day was etched on their brains like the scratch of a pin. The horror, the grief, and ultimately the triumph and the relief. Their father, Will, was interviewed by the police, poked and prodded at the hospital, and sent home. The local newspaper reported on his miraculous reappearance six years after he had gone missing from the same shore.

At first he couldn't process what had happened to him and took to his bed.

'What's the last thing you remember?' they asked him.

'Sitting on the shore, fishing. That's it.'

'You didn't see a horse?'

'A horse? No.'

They didn't push him. Ella did lie in the bed next to him; he took her face in his hands and stared into her eyes in wonder and sadness. 'I feel like I only saw you the other day, so small. But another part of me feels like I've missed so much,' he said.

'And we've missed *you*.' She put her arm across his chest and burrowed in, smelling his jersey smell, feeling his beardy face in her hair.

Fiona hung back. He beckoned her forward and she moved, one step at a time, slowly. She stood beside the bed, staring, as if not quite trusting that he wasn't a vision, a changeling, that would soon disappear in a puff of smoke.

'What do you think happened to him?' Morag asked when Will was finally sleeping in the other room and they sat close together on the couch. 'How can he have survived for so long?'

Fiona speculated that maybe he was with the faerie folk for six years. That he had been protected by a bubble in the lake. That his body had been suspended and his mind put to sleep. Or that he had time-travelled; that it really had been no time at all.

Ella knew. She couldn't explain it to them, but in the fleeting glimpses Gus had laid in her mind she had sensed him there, suspended, as Fiona said, just out of reach, outside time. She would never know why the kelpie hadn't drowned her father, or the children. Or Olive.

Unlike the rest of them, her father looked no older than the day he had left. He had touched Morag's hair in wonder at its whiteness.

'You know I used to dye it, right?' she said.

'But that was for a bit of salt and pepper, not this.' He dropped it, rubbed her shoulder. 'I like it; it suits you. You don't half look like your mother though.'

They all fell silent then.

'Grizzly had cancer,' said Fiona. 'She was going to die.'

'And how did that make you feel, little one?' Will reached out to touch her, and she leaned away, but then changed her mind and took his hand and pressed it to her cheek.

'If I painted a picture, it would be blue, blue, dark blue, a whirlpool, with a little stick figure caught in the middle.'

Will looked puzzled for a moment but seemed to catch on.

'And when you thought you'd lost me?'

Fiona and Ella looked at each other. Ella nodded, and said, 'A big black horse against a grimmeling sky.'

GRIZZLY HADN'T WANTED any fuss for her funeral. Family. Rita and Hana. The very few friends who had seen her for the person she was, not the person the town had painted her as — eccentric, prickly, suspicious even. A troublemaker. A witch. But Ella realised that perhaps they had been right to fear her, to fear all of them: they brought the kelpie here, and the town nearly lost its children because of them. Even if they couldn't remember it.

They put a notice in the newspaper but they didn't expect any more than a handful of people to come. They had no body to bury after all. But they had to do something, even just for themselves. Grizzly wasn't religious, not in the usual sense, but she had loved that old stone church on the hill in the middle of the paddock, with a roof that leaked and the rafters filled with nesting birds. She even loved the sheep that regularly charged in, leaving their droppings behind. Fiona wanted to decorate it as if for a party, and Morag let her, buying the things she needed, the streamers, the balloons. They swept up the sheep poo and scrubbed the pews.

On the morning of the funeral, they saddled the horses. Fiona and Ella plaited ribbons into their manes and tails, and Will strapped his violin to his back. The girls wore dresses and dirty boots. Hana wore her best pink jodhpurs, and Will and Morag wore bush shirts in honour of Grizzly's preferred choice of clothing. Duke sported her old battered sunhat, with holes cut for his ears, and didn't mind in the least. They made their way in procession up to the church: Morag on Olive, Will on Sir Ed, Hana on Duke, Fiona on Peedie, and Ella on Magpie. They trotted over paddocks now swollen with lambs, which skipped out of their way and took refuge behind their mothers. Rita greeted them at the door of the church — she had preferred to drive up the rough road on the other side.

They turned the horses out into the neighbouring paddock, but while the other horses eagerly searched for new grass, Magpie called to Ella over the fence.

'Come on, Ellie,' said Morag. 'It's time.'

'Just a minute!' She returned to her pony, planted a kiss on her nose and fondled her ears. 'You're a wonder, you know that?' Magpie nudged her and Ella laughed. Yes, she knew it. How much could she understand about what had happened? And what would their life be like together now that she knew that Magpie was half kelpie? She had a feeling that nothing much would change, even though everything had.

She hurried into the church after giving Magpie a last kiss on the crescent moon beneath her forelock. Her family waited at the front: Morag, Fiona, Will, Rita and Hana, all sitting in the first pew. When she sat down, Will stood up and lifted his violin to his chin. He played a sweet, sawing song that twisted through the air. Ella recognised it as the lament that Grizzly had sung by the lake, and her eyes filled with tears.

The doors clunked open, and when they turned Grizzly's friend Sue Kim, from the bookshop, was there. She nodded at them, embarrassed, and hurried to one of the middle pews to sit down. The door clunked shut again. Will played on, building to a crescendo, then stopped. In the silence, the door opened again. Once again, they turned to look. It was Susan, and Josh, and Josh's father Ross. Susan was holding Josh's hand; he was nearly as tall as she was and stood stiffly by her. His father pushed him forward and the family moved uncertainly into the church. Morag stood.

'You are welcome,' she said.

Ross nodded, and gave a sort of grunt, and they filed into a pew a few rows back, still keeping their distance.

Ella closed her eyes, feeling the familiar guilt bubble up, but she swallowed it down, turned and smiled at Josh. He lifted a hand, then put it in his pocket, blushing. Later, he would tell her about the day he rode the most magnificent horse he'd ever seen, but he didn't remember what happened after that.

Morag moved to the pulpit, as if she was a minister about to address the congregation.

But before she could speak, the door opened yet again. It was little Anahera and her mother; behind her there were more people. They moved solemnly down the aisle: Anahera, her mother, Ella's classmate Sylvie and her parents, and more families — the children the kelpie had taken, with their parents, their brothers and sisters, their grandparents. The families who said they could not remember and yet here they were. It didn't stop with them. Ella stood and watched in amazement as more and more people filed into the church. Her teacher Miss Coupland, her classmate Naz and her parents, the butcher, the librarian, Tim the school bus driver, the town's mayor. Hana leapt up when her mother and her three younger brothers came in, and beckoned them to sit with her, shuffling along to make room. The townspeople filled the pews, scooting to the very edges and squeezing into every available space. When the pews were filled, and more people came, they hovered at the back of the church.

Will stood with his violin dangling in his hand beside him, weeping silently. Fiona put her arms around Ella's waist, and Ella put hers around her sister's shoulders. They watched as the crowd stopped moving and became still, expectant. The door closed for the last time.

'What's this?' Fiona said quietly. She had put her hand inside the pocket of Ella's coat, the one she only wore for best, and pulled out a torn piece of paper. They looked at it together, reading the word written on it, and the definition.

Ella squeezed Fiona's hand as Morag, her eyes glistening, began.

'My mother, Griselda, came to this country for a better life, bringing a little bit of her beloved Scotland with her.'

As she listened to her mother's words, Ella looked up, just as a *glisk* of sunlight dropped through the clouds and

289

the hole in the roof, lighting the bright colours of Fiona's looping streamers and silver balloons. A perching magpie leaned over, one curious eye taking them in, shook itself, and fanned its wing as if in greeting.

'Thank you,' she whispered.

*Midsummer: summer solstice;
the longest day of the year*

'Higher!' called Ella, watching the flames dance.

'All right, miss bossy pants,' said her father. 'We don't want to set fire to everything in the vicinity.'

The midsummer bonfire crackled against the still evening air. It was past nine o'clock and the grimmelings were holding steady, a fiery line on the horizon. The first stars pricked the sky.

Earlier, Will and Morag and other parents had rowed the local children out to throw flowers on the surface of the lake. All of them wore colourful wreaths in their hair. Fiona had instructed them on how to make them,

291

using the pink and purple lupins that brought splashes of intense colour to the lakeside and the golden landscape every summer. They'd spent a joyous afternoon, with the whole community showing up with armfuls of blooms. She'd told them that today was the day the faeries and the spirits could make contact, and Ella knew that deep down she was hoping that Grizzly would return. But the lake remained blue and breeze-dimpled, and even the keld was refusing to give up its secrets.

If the kelpie was still in the lake, today of all days it would surely return. But it had gone, banished by their grandmother for good.

They'd brought the horses down, too. Ella threaded flowers through Magpie's reins, and made her a flower crown, which she accepted with good grace. Her friend Sylvie rode Zippy, who of course refused to go in the lake, but Sylvie was getting better at riding every week and would soon graduate to a livelier mount, one that didn't mind getting its feet wet. There were adventures to be had, and even Magpie seemed to approve of her.

Later, everyone gathered around a fire in the stone circle, drinking and eating from the hāngī that Hana's brothers had laid in the ground earlier in the day to emerge steaming — mutton and carrots, and potatoes hot and buttery. Ella sat next to Will, the chief fire warden, and on the other side Morag leaned into him, her eyes closed and a small smile on her lips. Ella had never seen her look so unruffled.

Fiona was off somewhere, playing with her newfound friends. Ella, too, had found herself more popular once school went back after the spring holidays. The locals no longer avoided them. *They will always think we're a bit weird*, thought Ella, *but I'm okay with that.*

'Dad!' Fiona appeared breathless behind them. She grabbed his hand and leaned back, pulling him. 'Come on!'

Will lost his balance and fell off the log, laughing, while Morag moved away to avoid being hit by his flying feet.

'Okay, okay!' He heaved himself up, but Fiona had already skipped over to Anahera and her other friends, who stood waiting in anticipation like a band of pixies, their eyes shining in the firelight beneath their flower crowns.

Will crouched low, stretched out his arms and bellowed. He stomped wide-legged towards the girls, who screamed and scattered, grinning, tumbling over and picking themselves up again. This time, nobody seemed to mind that Will was scaring the children, and Ella wondered if they'd ever remember what happened to them that day on the lake when they were nearly lost.

Will grabbed Fiona and threw her high in the air, catching her and falling on the ground with her safe in his arms. Her laugh was like music in the twilight.

'Hello, you lot.' It was Hana, grinning, her hair sticking up even higher than usual, glowing purple. 'I want to introduce you to someone.'

A young woman stepped out from her shadow and waved awkwardly. 'Hello.'

Morag sat up straighter and gave a small gasp.

'What?' said Ella. 'What is it?'

'The thing is,' said Hana, 'Cara's over here from Scotland for a sort of working holiday.' She looked at her toes, scuffing them in the grass. 'And I sort of said you might be looking for someone to help out around the place.'

Morag stood up. She leaned in and looked at the girl's face closely. She had large, wideset eyes, a high forehead and thick brown hair, parted in the middle.

'Cara, you say? It's remarkable. Will!'

Will released Fiona, slippery as a fish, and came back into the circle of light. 'You called?'

'Can you see it?' She flicked her head in Cara's direction.

'I can,' he said. 'Remarkable,' he agreed.

'What is it?' said Hana, as her friend took a step back, looking slightly alarmed.

'Forgive me, Cara,' said Morag. 'You must think I'm mad. Please sit. Shuffle over, Ellie.'

Cara and Hana sat. Ella, further out, could already feel the air cooling as the fire died down.

'The thing is,' said Morag, 'you look the spitting image of my mother, the girls' grandmother. They called her—'

'Grizzly!' Fiona stood in front of them, hopping from one foot to another. 'We called her Grizzly.'

'Well,' said Cara. 'Hello, little one!' Her Scottish accent wrapped itself around Ella like a warm blanket. 'My friends do call me Granny. Don't ask.'

'Granny!' Ella looked sideways at Morag, who was still squinting at Cara in the flickering light. 'Why Granny?'

'I did tell you not to ask, but I suppose it's because I'm an old soul. And I like an early night with a hot water bottle.' She laughed and the fire grew brighter for a moment. A glisk.

Fiona clambered onto Hana's knee so she could sit next to Cara. 'Where you come from, is there a lake?'

'Aye, a beautiful loch. A bit like this one.'

'And have you left a great love, and might he follow you down here?'

'Ach, no, child! What a question. I don't need a man, anyway.' She cast a glance at Hana then, who blushed and looked away, pleased.

Hana changed the subject. 'Cara grew up on a farm, Morag. She's got heaps of experience with horses.'

'And with kids,' added Cara.

'Well,' said Morag, 'I can see you'd fit in. What do you think, Fifi?'

Fiona nodded vigorously.

'Ellie? It might be nice to have a Scottish accent in the house again.'

Ella had a good feeling about this Cara. 'Definitely.' She smiled shyly.

'We can't pay you much, but we can give you room and board in return for you helping out every now and then? Looking after the kids and sometimes the horses?'

'That's great,' said Cara. 'Really. Just for a few months. I'd love to have an excuse to hang out in this beautiful part of the world. It has a magical feeling.'

Fiona took her by the hand. 'That's because it's a thin place,' she said.

Cara's eyebrows arched. 'Is it now? How wonderful. I'm looking forward to having some adventures with you.'

'Not too many adventures,' said Morag. 'Our family's had quite enough to last a lifetime.'

'You speak the truth,' said Will. 'Come on, let's shut this party down and get you girls to bed.'

'No,' they said in unison. 'A song! One more song.'

'One more,' agreed Will. He picked up his violin and began to play. It was a swooping, stomping, rhythmic tune, and soon people were up on their feet and dancing. The irresistible song reminded Ella of galloping horses. She grabbed Fiona by the hands and swung her around and around, stamping her feet and throwing her head back to the night.

Up on the hill, the horses moved against the very last glimmer of light. Magpie lifted her head and let out a whinny that carried down towards the fire. It swirled around Ella, then passed over her to the lake, where it slipped under its surface and eddied in the deep like a secret.

An deireadh: the end

ACKNOWLEDGEMENTS

I am extremely grateful to Creative New Zealand for a grant to write this book. After eight years in a creatively and emotionally demanding job, being given the time to write was priceless.

Thanks to the Michael King Writers Centre for a blissful two-week residency that kickstarted the book at the end of 2020.

Huge thanks to Jenny Hellen, Abba Renshaw, Leanne McGregor and the rest of the team at Allen & Unwin New Zealand for welcoming me into the family and for embracing me so wholeheartedly. Thank you to Jane Parkin for your sensitive editing; I've loved working with you. Thank you to Max Thompson for the utterly beautiful and arresting cover illustration that captures the tone of the story so well — I love it — and to Katrina Duncan for the gorgeous design.

Thank you to the fantastic team at Guppy Books — Bella Pearson, Hannah Featherstone and Catherine Alport — for giving *The Grimmelings* such a warm home away from home.

Thank you to my wonderful agent Gaia Banks at Sheil Land Associates for your support and guidance and championing, and to my previous agent Vivien Green, who looked after me so well even through the years I wasn't actually writing.

Thank you to Tania Roxborogh (Ngāti Porou) — our regular writing dates and chats at Tūranga were essential in writing this book. Ella and Charlie will be forever entwined. Your suggestions and advice on te reo use were invaluable.

Kā mihi to Juanita Hepi (Kāi Tahu, Waitaha, Kāti Māmoe, Ngāti Mutunga, Moriori, Ngāti Kahungunu, Ngāti Wai, Ngāpuhi) for your sensitive reading and clear-eyed advice, and for your treasured support and friendship. I'm so glad to have met you.

Thanks to Duncan McLean for checking my Scottish granny rang true, to Stacy Gregg for encouragement with my horses, to writing buddy Rachael Craw for cheer-leading, and to Elizabeth Knox for reading the book at a crucial stage and offering wise advice and friendship.

Thank you to my enthusiastic first young readers,

Matilda Grainger and Sylvie Woods. Special thanks to Sylvie for her help coming up with various names, personalities, colouring and quirks for my band of horses, making them gallop off the page.

Thank you to Jan Priestley and Bronwyn Hayward for providing me with two spaces to write and think on Banks Peninsula when I needed them most.

I wanted to write a novel for children that turned them on to the joys of language as well as adventure. I'm indebted to Robert Macfarlane, who I do not know, but whose 'Word of the Day' on Twitter inspired the language and title of *The Grimmelings* and led me to reading *Landmarks*. Many of the words and definitions that Grizzly teaches Ella come from that wonderful book (read it!) or from the *Dictionaries of the Scots Language* online (dsl.ac.uk).

I want to thank the creators of the Backlisted podcast, which was a weekly balm in the incredibly stressful couple of years of 2020/2021, and which made me want to be not only a better reader but a better writer. I thank them for taking children's books seriously in the books they feature on the podcast and in the guests they choose. Listening to the discussion around children's books sent me off down many a path of thinking deeply about stories and how to tell them.

I acknowledge the huge influence of Susan Cooper on my work. Reading *The Dark is Rising* series as a twelve-year-old shaped my worldview and therefore the adult I became. For years I was haunted by an image of someone standing on the edge of a lake, shouting at a monster within. This became my climactic scene. Imagine my surprise when I reread *Silver on the Tree* and there is the same image, with Bran shouting at the *afanc*. I had carried it around all these years believing it to be my own. I hope Susan Cooper forgives me.

The episode about *The Dark is Rising* on Backlisted was a tonic. Robert Macfarlane said: 'Language is magic . . . it has power. We utter it for good or ill . . . and these books are full of . . . the magical powers of language, spoken language, read.' He also went on to say, 'We're all exiles from our childhoods . . . looking back into the country we can't cross the border into.' This is my attempt to recross that border with all the knowledge and experience I have as a backward-looking adult, meeting my forward-yearning younger self just over the threshold.

Mythologist Martin Shaw's extraordinary *Courting the Wild Twin* brought me profoundly closer to my story and characters in ways I can't explain and possibly can't understand. Poet Robin Robertson's 'invented Scots folk narratives' are with me always.

Thank you as ever to the Brunette Mafia, who have been my biggest emotional support outside family for twenty years; to Claire Mabey and Gerri Judkins for nourishing chats about children's books; to my writing roommate Nic Low; and to my book club mates, especially Naomi and Erin — you transformed my social life in Christchurch and placed a love of books even more firmly at the centre.

Lastly, thanks and love to my whole wide family, especially Peter, Taylor and AJ.

PHOTO BY MATT BIALOSTOCKI

Rachael King is a writer, reviewer and former literary festival director from Aotearoa New Zealand. She loves music and started playing bass guitar in rock bands when she was fifteen, but these days spends more time listening. When Rachael was young she tried to ride every horse she met and could often be found galloping bareback along a beach with the wind in her hair. *The Grimmelings* is her second book for children; the first, *Red Rocks*, won the Esther Glen Medal in 2013 and is in development for television. Both novels reflect her love for, and obsession with, Scottish folklore — the weirder the better. Rachael has also published two novels for adults.

www.rachael-king.com

GUPPY
BOOKS

Guppy Books is an independent children's publisher based in Oxford in the UK, publishing exceptional fiction for children of all ages.

Small and responsive, inclusive and communicative, Guppy Books was set up in 2019 and publishes only the very best authors and illustrators from around the world.

From funny illustrated tales for five-year-olds and magical middle-grade stories, to inspiring and thought-provoking novels for young adults, Guppy Books promises to publish something for everyone. If you'd like to know more about our authors and books, go to the Guppy Aquarium on YouTube where you'll find interviews, draw-alongs and all sorts of fun.

Bella Pearson
Publisher

www.guppybooks.co.uk